# SPECIAL SUBSCRIPTION OFFER!
## For New Subscribers

*Subscribe and receive a free back issue
from our archives!*

*(offer expires August 1, 1987)*

. . . . . . . . . . . . . . . . . . . . . . . . . . . . . . . . . . . . . . . . . . . . . . . . . . . . . . . . .

### SUBSCRIBE NOW!

**CALYX**
P.O. Box B
Corvallis, OR 97339

☐ *Yes, I would like the International
Issue for $6 with my subscription*

☐ Please check if renewal
☐ 1 year           $18
☑ 2 years         $32
☐ 3 years         $42
☐ library/institution    $22.50
☐ low income individual    $15

add $4 per year foreign surface postage
$9 per year foreign air mail postage

_____
name

_____
address

_____
city        state        zip

Begin my subscription with (check one): ☐ current issue   ☐ next issue

A gift card to read from: _____

*Please enclose your check with your subscription*

. . . . . . . . . . . . . . . . . . . . . . . . . . . . . . . . . . . . . . . . . . . . . . . . . . . . . . . . .

# INTERNATIONAL ISSUE
## October 1980 - February 1981, Volume V, #2 & 3

For copies of this unique collection return this form with $8.50 per issue for individuals, or $11 for institutions plus postage and handling overseas. Mail to: CALYX, P.O. Box B, Corvallis, OR 97339.

_____
name

_____
address

_____
city      state      zip

Ship____ copies at     $ _____

Plus Postage *($1.50 surface,* $ _____
*$5 air each, Overseas)*

*Total enclosed*     $ _____

# SUPPORT THE WORK OF CREATIVE WOMEN!
# BECOME A MATRON OF THE ARTS!

. . . . . . . . . . . . . . . . . . . . . . . . . . . . . . . . . . .

## DONATE NOW!
## HELP CALYX AS A
## CONTRIBUTING SUPPORTER.

CALYX
P.O. Box B
Corvallis, OR 97339-0539

DONOR
____$25
____$26-$99
MATRON
____$100
____$150 or more

_____
name

_____
address

_____
city                          state                          zip

Include my name as a contributing supporter in the next issue
of CALYX. _____yes _____no.

*All contributions are tax deductible. CALYX is a nonprofit corporation with a 501C (3) status.*

*Thank you!*

. . . . . . . . . . . . . . . . . . . . . . . . . . . . . . . . . . .

A volunteer editorial board produces CALYX, the ONLY WEST COAST PUBLI-
CATION OF ITS KIND. You can help ensure that women's voices continue to be
published by supporting the work of CALYX through a donation. Contributors
help ensure that production costs can be met despite increasing postal rates and
cuts in grant supporting agencies. DONATE NOW and Matronize the arts!

The editors regret the recent rise in subscription and single copy rates. The current
economy and the doubling of production costs necessitate the increase. The last
subscription increase was in 1978 from $5 to $10. Please note we offer a special
subscription rate of $15 to low income individuals.

# FLORILEGIA

Grateful acknowledgment is made to the following for permission to reprint the following copyrighted material:

Guri Andermann, "Syllogisms" reprinted in *Soundings East*, Vol. 6#2, 1983, copyright © 1983 by Guri Andermann; Ellen Bass, "Even This" reprinted in *Our Stunning Harvest* (New Society Publishers) copyright © 1981 by Ellen Bass; Olga Broumas, "Amazon Twins" and "Song/For Sanna" reprinted in *Beginning With O* (Yale University Press) copyright © 1977 by Olga Broumas; Jan Clausen, "Yellow Jackets" reprinted in *Mother, Sister, Daughter, Lover* (The Crossing Press) copyright © 1980 by Jan Clausen; Jane Hirshfield, "The Stream Of It" reprinted in *Alaya* (The Quarterly Review of Literature Poetry Series) copyright © 1983 by Jane Hirshfield; Linda Hogan, "Crow" reprinted in *Iris*, Fall 1985, copyright © 1985 by Linda Hogan; Darlene Mathis-Eddy, "Widow's Walk" reprinted in *Leaf Threads, Wind Rhymes* (Barnwood Press) copyright © 1985 by Darlene Mathis-Eddy; Sharon Olds, "The Language Of The Brag" reprinted in *Satan Says* (University of Pittsburgh Press) copyright © 1980 by Sharon Olds; Pat Mora, "*Bruja*/Witch" originally appeared in *Chants* (Arte Publico Press, 1984) copyright © 1984 by Pat Mora.

*Calyx* publishes three issues in each annual volume. Subscription rates for individuals are: $18/1 year; $32/2 years; $42/3 years. Library and institution subscription rate: $22.50/1 year. A special subscription rate of $15/1 year is available to low-income individuals. Add $4/year for foreign postage surface rate, $9/year for foreign postage air rate. Single copy prices are: $6.50 for single issues and $12 for double issues. Add $1 postage for each issue. Address all correspondence to: *Calyx*, P.O. Box B, Corvallis, OR, 97339. (503) 753-9384.

*Calyx, A Journal Of Art And Literature By Women* is archived in the University of Oregon Library, Eugene, Oregon.

*Calyx, A Journal Of Art And Literature By Women* is indexed in *American Humanities Index* and *Alternative Press Index*.

**SUBSCRIBER CHANGE OF ADDRESS:** Please notify *Calyx* promptly of any address changes. Bulk mail is not forwarded and each issue returned to *Calyx* costs $2 and upward to claim and reship (if the Post Office can give us a new address). If we don't hear from you when you move, we both lose, so please, DON'T FORGET TO SEND CHANGE OF ADDRESS FORMS!

# CALYX

## A JOURNAL OF ART AND LITERATURE BY WOMEN

### *FLORILEGIA, A RETROSPECTIVE, 1976-1986*

*Spring 1987*

## volume 10 numbers 2 and 3

*Managing Editors:* Margarita Donnelly, Lisa Domitrovich;
*Managing Editor Art:* Debi Berrow; *Editors:* Catherine Holdorf,
Barbara Loeb (art), Susan Lisser, Cheryl McLean, Carol Pennock,
Linda Varsell Smith; *Volunteers:* Gea Barker, Barbara Hadley,
Abbie McCormick, Ingrid McCutcheon, Emily Whitlock.

*Associate Editors:* Jo Alexander, Rebecca Gordon,
Meredith Jenkins, Ingrid Wendt, Eleanor Wilner.

*Cover*
Debi Berrow

# FLORILEGIA

## CONTENTS

*ART*

## PROSE

## ESSAYS

## CONTRIBUTORS' NOTES

*T*he calyx is the protective covering on the flowerbud. The bud blossoms as the calyx opens and falls away. The flower in all its magnificence becomes the centerpiece of the plant. Its beauty, color, and fragrance attract the bee and the butterfly so that it can fruit and seed and bring forth new life.

**Florilegia:** *a culling of flowers; anthologies of writings.*

This retrospective covers the first decade of publishing (1976-1986) by *Calyx, A Journal of Art and Literature by Women. Calyx* was founded on the belief that a female aesthetic in literature and art exists and that it could be better seen and nurtured by publishing women's work in the context of other women's work. In *Florilegia* a new group of editors reexamines this premise with the publication of 96 artists and writers whose works are representative of the important issues, forms, styles, and visions published during *Calyx's* first decade.

This retrospective is not a "best of"; we do not want women's work to be seen in terms of competition where one work is placed above another. Instead, this anthology represents a collective expression of women's realities, visions, and dreams—our voices blending to dispute a "reality" defined by a limited elite that excludes our perceptions.

In the selection process we requested assistance from past editors and associate editors. Eleanor Wilner, a contributing editor, eloquently defined our intent in her response:

*. . . when I think of* Calyx, *I think of people, of themes, of paths—as if, out on the snow fields of Reagan's frozen tundra, we were making deep tracks for each other, so that it's impossible to say "she went that way first" or "those are her prints," but only that the path is there, there are safe houses along the way, we're going together. This is, for me, feminism's best self, the positive*

*form of that old female anonymity; here, it is a chosen anonymity, a conversation in which everyone has her own voice. I hardly notice the names at the end of poems, but I remember lines, images—the "scared sheep/blubbering 'Faa-ther, Faa-ther'" as Abraham leaves with his son, the sacrifice; the five-year-old girl who is the revolution, who is picked up, swung high in the air, loved and looked after by one person after another—"a barefoot sun in dungarees. Any/one of us would do these things." That's it. That's what's missing in mainstream America, and in the world of letters too—a vanity-trap if there ever was one . . . The consequence of all this is not a show-case but a kind of tapestry we all are weaving (with the . . . accompaniment of the conversation that is part of the process of its creation).*

In *Florilegia* the conversation continues—the murmurs of women's histories weave back and forth, women nurturing each other's work—ideas intertwine between genera-tions, passing from mother to daughter, from woman to woman—in "women's do-main"—an open space that remains mysteriously invisible to men who never dally long enough to hear or see the world in which women live.

Women's creative work is often rendered invisible or impotent—sometimes through lack of documentation, loss or misrepresentation (works by women under male names), or, most common, through rejection and miscomprehension. Many works have survived only to become nameless. Because of this we say, "Anonymous was a woman." In *Florilegia* we celebrate the work of women who are no longer anonymous or invisible, and we remember that our *her*story includes "Anonymous." She is everywhere; her work feeds us. We celebrate her strength, her will to contemplate upon her existence, and her ability to survive despite the odds.

*Florilegia* offers the creative thinking of a female consciousness that in its critical reflection may present an impetus for action, a spark in the darkness lighting a new path. In the work presented interrelationships can be found between patriarchal atti-tudes toward that which is female and patriarchal attitudes toward mother earth. We expose the terror and our struggle, while celebrating the transforming powers of survi-val and the sublime. The intricacies and drudgery of daily life form the background from which we delineate the importance of "our" domain, a domain in which "the per-sonal *is* political."

# THE LANGUAGE OF THE BRAG

I have wanted excellence in the knife-throw,
I have wanted to use my exceptionally strong and accurate arms
and my straight posture and quick electric muscles
to achieve something at the center of a crowd,
the blade piercing the bark deep,
the haft slowly and heavily vibrating like the cock.

I have wanted some epic use for my excellent body,
some heroism, some American achievement
beyond the ordinary for my extraordinary self,
magnetic and tensile, I have stood by the sandlot
and watched the boys play.

I have wanted courage, I have thought about fire
and the crossing of waterfalls, I have dragged around

my belly big with cowardice and safety,
my stool black with iron pills,
my huge breasts oozing mucus,
my legs swelling, my hands swelling,
my face swelling and darkening, my hair
falling out, my inner sex
stabbed again and again with terrible pain like a knife.
I have lain down.

I have lain down and sweated and shaken
and passed blood and feces and water and
slowly alone in the center of a circle I have
passed the new person out
and they have lifted the new person free of the act
and wiped the new person free of that
language of blood like praise all over the body.

I have done what you wanted to do, Walt Whitman,
Allen Ginsberg, I have done this thing,
I and the other women this exceptional
act with the exceptional heroic body,
this giving birth, this glistening verb,
and I am putting my proud American boast
right here with the others.

*SHARON OLDS*
*Vol. 2#2, 1977*

## ARGUING WITH JOYCE

We are all out there on the edge without parachutes
and it is no picnic and the edge keeps moving towards
us and receding again until the eyes and the feet and
the stomach have no guarantee they're related. There is
only one rule, you can't move backwards, so it's only
a question of whether the edge will meet you before
you meet it. Any woman who yells, *No one understands!*
is a fool. There is no woman who doesn't understand.
It is a prism of understanding. You stand on an edge
that cuts while I stand on a surface that burns, you
stand on Route 128 unable to move your car yelling
to the rain which is deaf as well as mute and I yell
to the strep in my daughter's throat which makes a
statement of pus. Either way, no one arrives on a
white horse, no one even sends help. You call for a
tow and hitch to work drenched, I stay at home for
the fourth day in a row. The edge wavers again. When
it finally happens, nothing will matter. Your Saab
with its cracked block, nursing my daughter back to
health, getting your budget in before June, getting
my poems out before I land, forgetting to write our
wills. It all happened so fast, we'll say, We saw it
coming for years, the race, the edge, the air, the
free fall, this falling free and we are all howling
in the green air. Howling with laughter.

*JUDITH W. STEINBERGH*
*Vol. 7#3, 1983*

# SYLLOGISMS

> *And I find more bitter than death*
> *the woman, whose heart is snares*
> *and nets, and her hands as bands.*
> Ecclesiastes 7:26

If a woman offers her heart, simple as glass,
and man sees a net, falls in
clean as a fish,
whom will he blame?

If a woman offers her heart
to a man who thinks only of snares,
will it pull his bowels out of him,
ruined and limp?

If a woman offers her hand
to a man who can be bound by fingers,
will she listen as he breaks them,
watch as they fall to the floor?

If a woman offers her hand
to a man who is always screaming,
she might put her hands to her ears,
might take his tongue off at the root.

I find more bitter than death
the man who believes something vital
folds out of him, silk from a parachute,
the man who believes he will be lost and falling
in the open sky of a woman.

*GURI ANDERMANN*
*Vol. 7#3, 1983*

POET

*(for Nancy, who ceased to write
when her professor told her she
had the words of a housewife)*

In the works of other poets Erika had read
the cadence of *immanent* and *inexorable,*
read *explosion* and *catharsis.*
But when she turned to her work table,
bent her back, Erika quietly nudged her pencil.
She had words as small and contained
as the unopened buds on a shaft of broccoli.

The frugality of her meals
had taught her this spareness of language.
She felt the lilt of her forearm
as she chopped carrots, parsley.
Barley rocked in boiling water.
The pungence of basil searched the air, questioned,
What is poetry?
The simpleness of rosemary, of oregano answered,
Poetry is rhythm and image and meaning.

Night rose. Poems murmured at Erika's fingertips,
trellised up her arms.
She watered the coleus,
called her children to bed.
Then, in the stillness of her room,
in anonymity, Erika wrote;
John, with this sentence I record my years.
Even the straight jacket of its rind
cannot restrain the grapefruit's final burgeoning,
the sections unfolding.
And who is to say this language is not enough?

*ALEXA HOLLYWOOD*
*Vol. 4#3, 1980*

## THE STREAM OF IT

They might say, *a white bird in the snow,*
and study it for years.
When the lacquer bucket breaks,
water is everywhere.
But water already is everywhere,
& salt; this much I understand
or hope.

The binding shadow, orange,
of an orange peel;
sky painted through the hip of a cow.
What the painters learn is a river,
eye to hand,
the color of earth & mind the same,
& its shadow.
Still it's an unending struggle
to put it down,
even the best of them leaving
palettes like battlefields—
an unending struggle just to see what is,
when vision keeps breaking like water
across a stone, a constant rushing,
and light is a salmon,
always returning, blindly, to its source.

*JANE HIRSHFIELD*
*Vol. 7#2, 1982*

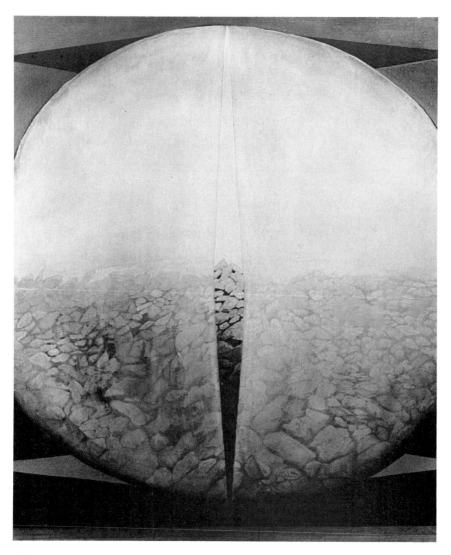

*Sphere*                    *acrylic*                  *FAEDRA KOSH*
                           *36" x 45"*
                        *Vol. 2#3, 1978*

*Alternate Way to Enter a Room*      CELESTE REHM
*acrylic*
*42" x 68"*
*Vol. 4#1, 1979*

*Descending Triangle*

*pastel on paper*
*40" x 36"*
Vol. 10#1, 1986
photo by David Reinert

*CAROL S. GATES*

*Ejemplo*                    *charcoal*                    ADA MEDINA
                          *30¼" x 22¼"*
                          *Vol. 8#2, 1984*

Cuento                    *black prismacolor pencil*                    *ADA MEDINA*
                              *22" x 18"*
                          *Vol. 4#2, 1979*

*Untitled*                                         *MELANIE TOLBERT*
*black and white photographs*
*Vol. 6#2, 1982*

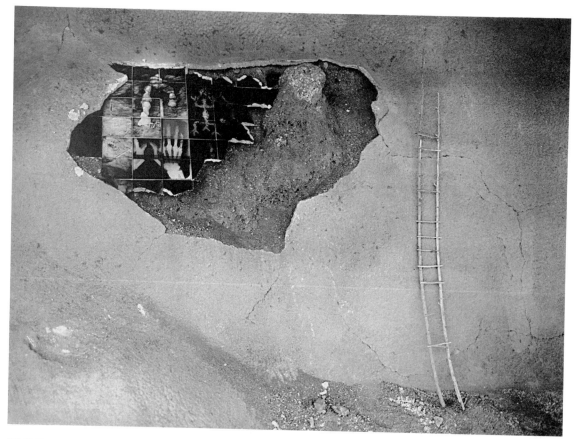

*Wall Fragment from Cliff Dwelling*     *black and white photograph*     ROBIN LASSER
*Vol. 6#2, 1982*

Swiss Barn                   *black and white photograph*                   ROBIN LASSER
                                  *Vol. 6#2, 1982*

*Megalithic Tomb Illumination*    *color photograph*    JOANNA PRIESTLEY
*Carrowkeel, Ireland*
*Vol. 7#2, 1982*

INANNA   ISHTAR   ISIS   IXCHEL   IO
HERA   DIANA   ATHENA   APHRODITE   ANNABEL
CAIA   MAAT   GEFJON   NEFTIS   NUT
FRIJA   FRIG   FREYA   FREJA   FORTUNA
DANU   ANU   BRIGIT   MACHA   NUAH   NEITH
AMATERSU   CIRCE   CETARARI   SOPHIA   RHEA
HECATE   SELKET   SELENE   PANDORA   MARY   MONA
LILITH   LILY   LUNA   SHEELA-NA-GIG

*The Day I Left My Vacuum Cleaner*      *appliqué*      PAULA KING
*Vol. 2#2, 1977*

*I*n *large-scale farming seedlings and young
plants are sprayed with toxic substances to eliminate unwanted life
forms. The once wild, multivaried and abundant garden is clipped and
tied, intensely cultivated, and ruthlessly weeded. Plant species are bred
into hybrids that lack resistance to the environment and depend on agri-
cultural methods that violate the symbiosis between plants and the earth.*

The oppression and denigration that women are subjected to is always a
part of our consciousness, but for too long it has existed without a name.
Women, whole races, cultures, nations, and the earth herself have been raped
by those in power. The story is the history of patriarchy and continues today.
All peoples and the planet are at serious risk from this disease.

In the following section women name the horror. They dissect it and expose it, revealing its implications. As we identify the oppressors and learn to
recognize the connections between sexism, racism, and the violation of the
planet and its life force, we become empowered and can begin the movement
to bring about a transformation.

*From* OEDIPUS DROWNED     *SHARON DOUBIAGO*

*7. How Do I Love Thee? Let Me Count The Ways*

*Male rule of the world has its emotic   l roots in female*
*rule of early childhood.*     Dorothy Dinnerstein

*I love my mother. I hate my mother....*
War: *That is what we have sons for....*
     *The Love and The Hate,* Robinson Jeffers


Now in his going out I go out with him and see:
In the infant's turning from the mother
lies culture's turning from the feminine.

                My son
                        so beautiful
                        so full of the sea, his soul

                Now he hears
                the father voices

                the ones who
                fearing love, fearing death
                fled me
                and nature

                the ones who, pursuing culture's authority:
                technology
                as revenge against nature
                as revenge against the mother
                        she
                        who brings us
                        through her body
                        into the carnal world
                        to death

                will make him their killer

                the ones who plan now
                the death of all

Man.
O, my Love.
I couldn't understand you.

*I couldn't understand the love of men*
*that diminishes with time*
*I couldn't understand the heart*
*that vows so easily and as easily breaks the vow*

*I couldn't understand*
*in that greatest love*
*the little boy's for his mother*

*the man's hatred — terror and humiliation —*
*of nature, of Earth*

*I couldn't understand*
*the death of the heart (the little boy's great heart)*
*I couldn't believe*
*the Death Wish*

*I couldn't understand*
*why*
*since we are of woman born*
*of woman raised*
*the world is not*
*a more erotic place*

*I couldn't understand*
*how*
*children raised by women*
*now and from all time and in all cultures*
*produce the patriarchy*

*I couldn't understand*
*war*
*how, now and always,*
*women raise the soldiers*

*why*
*we turn again and again*
*from freedom*
*to the despot*

*I couldn't understand*
*the stronger the mother*
*the stronger the military*

> *she makes life*
> *so he makes death*

But now my son is grown. Now
he hears
the father voices

> Now in my son's turning
>> in the sun's turning

> from me, his first act of self
>> the sun from the earth

> to find gender
> identity

>> for which I gave
>> my body and my soul

> he will always turn
> from my daughters

>> for which I gave
>> my body and my soul

> he will never
> be faithful

> commit himself
> wholly

> Even to the despot

always to the despot
from me, to death, to war and the fathers
now the sun from the earth

now the sun from progeny
granddaughter, great grandson

because the man
the father
second lover

will always seem
freedom

from the first God, the first tyrant
Mother

Now like Jeffers south of here
who rightfully
brings the stinking corpse of the boy
back from World War II
back to here, Earth's most erotic display of herself
to rape his mother
to kill his father
now I begin to see
the Love and the Hate

my son raised within and against
the history of our love.
You.
All my lovers.
On this edge.
I begin to see
his missing father

that sailor, that Russian, that Great Unknown
In The Sky, second love, second
God, that coward

In turning the sun from me
they will turn
the sun from Earth

My son

so beautiful, so full of me

My son

from out of me, this place, his soul
he now must drown

Now he hears the father voices
Now he bonds with all men
against me,
sister, mother, lover, daughter, Earth

Now he pulls out his eyes
so as not to see.  Now
we drown.

*SHARON DOUBIAGO*
*Vol. 10#1, 1986*

## ABRAHAM'S WIFE

Something afoot. The cattle
rumble and stamp. And the old man's
twitching bones rubbed him
so feverish I had to throw off
those burning sheets. I sat
and watched him as he stared
straight up into the dark
like a blind man, until he pulled
his drowning body out of the bed's
muddy waters. Then I recognized
that sleepwalker's look: another
man-made mystery: cut foreskin,
abused baby howling while the greybeards
grin, their limp tools atremble.

Now he bundles twigs and ties them
to the ass and shakes the boy
awake. I watch his gnarled feet
plod, thick as stumps,
dumb animals I'd like
to pound with my fists, beat senseless.
Even the ass won't balk
and the boy's obedient as the ass!
Like thieves or wolves, the three
sneak past the tent, the scared sheep
blubbering "Faa-ther, Faa-ther."
*Even if they come back,* my friend the moon
remarks over her shoulder,
*you've lost your son.*

*BETH BENTLEY*
*Vol. 4#3, 1980*

# DROWNING

I walk through my own shallows,
shivering over broken reflections:
how you coaxed me over my head.

Too slow. Too painful, this re-entry.
I back up, run full tilt at the waves,
dive in. Knowing
does not lessen the shock.

How the body adapts, rolls over,
gasps for air. I squint at the sun,
take a deep breath and pull down hard
towards the pressing deep.

Light filters in, its long angular strands.
Voices of pebbles and shells moan along the surge.
Salt seals my eyes. I surface, spouting.

You'd steal into my room at dawn, a grown
man climbing into the bed of his child.
I took to waking early, curled up, keeping
my back to the door, pretending sleep.
It never worked.

You uncurled me gently before first light.
Now I drown in the weight of resistance, the years
of silence, gagged into telling.

You loved me. I knew that.
Still, I lost a father.

The child, beyond saving, doesn't recover.
The mother she became storms the world, protective,
guarding her daughters and sons.

*ANNE YOUNG*
*Vol. 9#1, 1985*

EVEN THIS

My daughter
is five months old. I take her
with me to a slide presentation.
The room is darkened, she sleeps on a quilt.

The woman's voice is clipped, rushed
as she narrates. She has more facts
than time—
            children in pornographic magazines
            girls in suggestive advertising
            in films, child prostitutes
            children with venereal disease, babies
            three month old babies
            treated in hospitals
            for gonorrhea
            of the throat.

My baby sleeps, sucking
her thumb. She found her thumb
at three months.

When she wakes
she will suck my breast. The instinct
is strong, the muscles of the jaw, strong.
That first week, when my nipples were sore
she sucked my finger, her father's finger.
We laughed, startled by the power of her suck.

She sucks the ear of her rubber cat.
She greets the world with an open mouth.
A baby will suck anything.

Diseased men
put their penises
in babies' mouths.

The baby sucks. Sucking
is survival. A baby
lives by it.

*ELLEN BASS*
*Vol. 6#1, 1981*

## THE MENSTRUAL LODGE

Accepting the heavy destiny of power,
I went to the small house when the time came.
I ate no meat, looked no one in the eye,
and scratched my fleabites with a stick:
to touch myself would close the circle
that must be open so a man can enter.
After five days I came home,
having washed myself and all I touched and wore
in Bear Creek, washed away the sign,
the color, and the smell of power.

It was no use. Nothing,
no ritual or servitude or shame,
unmade my power, or your fear.

You waited in the thickets in the winter rain
as I went alone to the small house.
You beat my head and face and raped me
and went to boast. When my womb swelled,
your friends made a small circle with you:
    We all fucked that one.
    Who knows who's the father?

By Bear Creek I gave birth, in Bear Creek
I drowned it. Who knows who's the mother?
Its father was your fear of me.

I am the dirt beneath your feet.
What are you frightened of? Go fight your wars,
be great in club and lodge and politics.
When you find out what power is, come back.

I am the dirt, and the raincloud, and the rain.
The walls of my house are the steps I walk
from day of birth around the work I work,
from giving birth to day of death.
The roof of my house is thunder,
the doorway is the wind.
I keep this house, this great house.

When will you come in?

*URSULA K. LE GUIN*
*Vol. 10#1, 1986*

# REMEMBER THE MOON SURVIVES
## *BARBARA KINGSOLVER*

*for Pamela*

Remember the moon survives,
draws herself out crescent-thin,
a curved woman. Untouchable,
she bends around the shadow
that pushes itself against her, and she

waits. Remember how you waited
when the nights bled their darkness out
like ink, to blacken the days beyond,
to blind morning's one eye.
This is how you learned to draw
your life out like the moon,
curled like a fetus around the

shadow. Curled in your bed,
the little hopeful flowers of your knees
pressed against the wall
and its mockery of paint,
always the little-girl colors
on the stones of the ordinary prison:
the house where you are someone's
daughter, sister, someone's flesh, someone's

blood. The Lamb and Mary
have left you to float in this darkness
like a soup bone. You watch
the cannibal feast from a hidden place
and pray to be rid of your offering.
The sun is all you wait for,
the light, guardian saint of all the children
who lie like death on the wake

of the household crime. You stop
your heart like a clock: these hours
are not your own. You hide
your life away, the lucky coin
tucked quickly in the shoe
from the burglar, when he

comes. Because he will, as sure
as shoes. This is the one
with all the keys to where you live,
the one you can't escape, and while
your heart is stopped, he takes things.
It will take you years

to learn: why you hold back sleep
from the mouth that opens in the dark;
why you will not feed it with
the dreams you sealed up tight
in a cave of tears; why
the black widow still visits you,
squeezes her venom out in droplets,
stringing them like garnets
down your abdomen,
the terrifying jewelry of a woman
you wore inside, a child robbed

in the dark. Finally you know this.
You have sliced your numbness open
with the blades of your own eyes.
From your years of watching
you have grown the pupils of a cat, to see

in the dark. And these eyes are
your blessing. They will always know
the poison from the jewels that are both
embedded in your flesh.
They will always know the darkness
that is one of your names by now,
but not the one you answer to.
You are the one who knows, behind
the rising, falling tide
of shadow, the moon is always

whole. You take in silver
through your eyes, and hammer it
as taut as poems in steel
into the fine bright crescent of your life:
the sickle,
the fetus,
the surviving moon.

*BARBARA KINGSOLVER*
*Vol. 9#1, 1985*

# YOUR MOTHER'S EYES

*for Maura and Lesbia Lopez*

Maura, I have dreamed of your life:
there are lilies as red as blood, as a sunrise
that only grow from scarred earth after a fire.

Maura, your mother was sixteen,
without thoughts of you,
when they caught her painting walls,
painting the oldest kind of tomorrow
in colors she found only
inside her eyes.
When your mother was sixteen,
this was a crime.

Maura, she will never tell you everything
they did to her in prison: the men,
the pants tucked into boots, the pain.
The way she watched him
tuck his shirttail in
while she wondered what she would ever
find to love again.
Soon after this
she began to think of you.

Maura, there were people who said
you should not be born, that a life
conceived in hatred
is more hate than life.
Your mother said
the seed is the least of a tree
that has lived through several seasons.
Even before the first bud opens, the seed
is not what it was.
And so you were born
and in the season that brought you forth
they rang every bell in Nicaragua
all the way down to the sea
and promised kindness, the oldest
kind of tomorrow.
Even the men in boots
were treated with kindness.

Maura, you have your mother's eyes.

BARBARA KINGSOLVER
*Vol. 9#1, 1985*

# GUATEMALAN EXODUS: *LOS NATURALES*     *RENNY GOLDEN*

> *On the aspens of that land we hung up our*
> *harps . . . how could we sing a song to the Lord*
> *in a foreign land?*
> Psalm 137:2,4

I.

At night the Chiapas jungle
claps small hands
in a green wind of flutes,
shaking the *palmas* trees to music.
From high in *Huehuetenango*
they've walked, *niños* rocking
in *fusia* and scarlet back-slings.
*La gente's* possessions rolled in cloth packs,
carrying straw pouches of oat color.
With the first stars
they cross the border
breaking *Rio Suchiate's* black surface,
the women's traditional dress
spilling the river with bright flowers.
Near the bridge *la migra* with a slung rifle
watches downriver, scans toward *Union Juarez,*
a once-green refuge fire-bombed Holy Week
by Guatemalan air force scorching
the indolent countryside.

II.

> *I'm not killing the people. The devil has*
> *entered into the people. I'm killing the devil.*
>                                         Rios Montt

*Los indios* move into
a white mist clearing,
an apparition
of Guadalupe's children,
roses tumble from
the moon's silver cape.
These are what survived,
the unravelled weave of an Indian village,
blunt cut from an ancient bolt of land
that holds, now, the others;
their sweet bones, copper bodies,
broken, ashes.
Mothers, *campesinos* executed
in the town square,
children's eyes incredulous
as clubbed seal pups.
Their pelts, *sus padres*, all,
all to earth's scorched
and swollen arms.

III.

> *We wait for peace to no avail; for a time of*
> *healing and terror comes instead . . . over the*
> *mountains, break out in cries of lamentation,*
> *over the pasture lands intone a dirge; they are*
> *scorched and no man crosses them, unheard*
> *is the bleat of the flock; birds of the air, as*
> *well as beasts, all have fled and are gone.*
>                                    Jeremiah 8:15; 9:10

None of this is secret.
Not stone, but the *Altiplano* cries,
and her gentle people
cross one more border,
to the attics, not of Holland
but the United States,
hidden not from Nazis
but North American immigration
ready to deport them
back to an army
that kills for God.
Mayans in our midst, witnesses
to their nation's holocaust,
speaking in *Mam, Kanjobal, Kakchiquel,*
*Jacalteco, Quiche, Lacandon.*
Are we dreaming?
Are their tongues lost?
They show their scars,
photos of the burned villages.
Like Montt, US *migra*
calls upon the saints
and asks for further proof.
In this land we worship law,
even Cardinals bow down.
At the border, like a sea of blood,
the people wash into *Chiapas.*
The waves are relentless.

*RENNY GOLDEN*
*Vol. 8#3, 1984*

THE LAST MAN

—*for Vivian*

Here, in our familiar streets, the day
is brisk with winter's business.
The reassuring rows of brick façades,
litter baskets overflowing
with the harvest of the streets
and, when the light turns, the people
move in unison, the cars, miraculously,
slide to a stop, no one is killed,
the streets, for some reason, do not
show the blood that is pouring
like a tide, on other shores.

    Martinez, the last peasant left alive
    in his village, refuses to run, hopes
    that God, *El Salvador,*
    will let him get the harvest in.
    "Can a fish live out of water?" he says
    for why he stays, and weeds
    another row, ignoring the fins
    of sharks that push up
    through the furrows.

Here, it is said, we live
in the belly of the beast. Ahab sits
forever at the helm, his skin
white wax, an effigy. The whale carries
him, lashed to its side by the ropes
from his own harpoon. His eyes
are dead. His ivory leg
juts from the flank of Leviathan
like a useless tooth.

One more time, the little sail appears
a cloud forms, an old ikon for mercy
turned up in a dusty corner
of the sky, preparing rain
for the parched land, Rachel
weeping for her children. "Can a fish
live out of water?" he asks
and the rain answers, in Spanish,
*manitas de plata*
little hands of silver on his brow.

ELEANOR WILNER
*Vol. 8#3, 1984*

Black Birds          *black gouache*          GRAÇA MARTINS
                        *6" x 8¼"*
                     *Vol. 5#2&3, 1980*

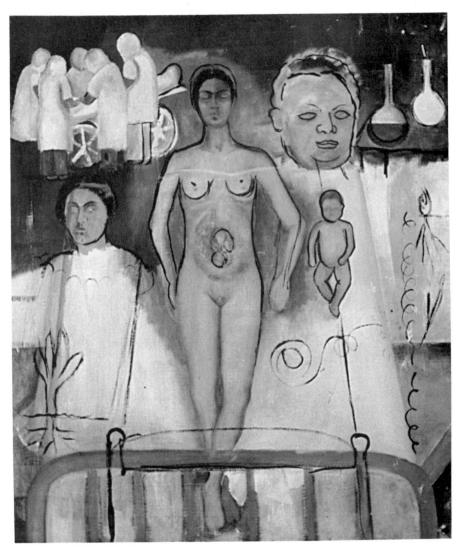

*Frida y la Cesarea*  *oil on canvas*  FRIDA KAHLO
24½" x 28¾"

*Vol. 5#2&3, 1980*
*photo by Nancy Deffebach*
*Collection of Museo Frida Kahlo, Mexico City*

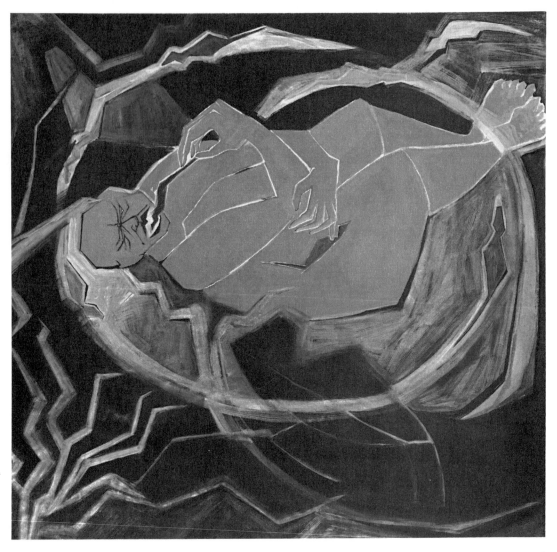

Communion                    tempera on paper          BARBARA THOMAS
                                48" x 48"
                             Vol. 8#3, 1984
                             photo by Chris Eden

*When Two Dance It's a Couple*       *BARBARA THOMAS*
*tempera on paper*
*36" x 72"*
*Vol. 8#3, 1984*
*photo by Chris Eden*

*The Patriotic Girls*
*Las muchachas patrioticas*

*assemblage*
*10" x 8"*
*Vol. 8#1, 1983*

KATHERINE GORHAM

*Small-Footed Ladies of the S.L.A.*
*Moments Before the End*

*pencil*
*25" x 16"*
*Vol. 5#2&3, 1980*

ZULEYKA BENITEZ

*Self-Portrait Series, #2*　　　　　　　　　*CAROLYN L. CÁRDENAS*
*egg/oil tempera on panel*
*7¾" x 9½"*
*Vol. 10#1, 1986*
Courtesy of Simard/Halm Gallery, Los Angeles

Night Life                *pencil/color pencil*                *CLAUDIA CAVE*
                                         *24" x 24"*
                                 *Vol. 7#1, 1982*

Pinky Gales          *black and white photograph*          PAULA ROSS
                          *Vol. 6#2, 1982*

*Self-Portrait as the Statue of Liberty*       ELIZABETH LAYTON
*color pencil and crayon on paper*
*22" x 30"*
*Vol. 9#2&3, 1986*

*I*n the ceaseless search for moisture and suste-
*nance, a plant's root system reaches widely and deeply beneath the dry
surface. The tap root may break through pipe, tile, even concrete, to get
to a source.*

The history of the planet and its peoples is a chronology of deletions and
amnesic episodes. A list of cataclysmic events, wars, colonizations. The real
events—everyday living, the connections between people, the stories of those
without power—are left out. They have been ignored, lost, and forgotten.

This section centers on our struggle for survival and the need to connect
to our lost past. Memories of our heritages and our *her*story surface from the
depth of a mutual consciousness.

# BAILING OUT—A POEM FOR THE 1970s

> *Whose woods these are I think I know.*
> Robert Frost

The landings had gone wrong; white silk,
like shrouds, covered the woods.
The trees had trapped the flimsy fabric
in their web—everywhere the harnessed bodies
hung—helpless, treading air
like water.             We thought to float down
easily—a simple thing
like coming home: feet first,
a welcome from the waiting fields,
a gentle fall in clover.

We hadn't counted on this
wilderness, the gusts of wind
that took us over; we were surprised
by the tenacity of branching wood,
its reach, and how impenetrable
the place we left, and thought we knew,
could be.             Sometimes now, as we sway, unwilling
pendulums that mark the time,
we still can dream
someone will come and cut us down.
There is nothing here but words, the calls
we try the dark with—hoping for a human
ear, response, a rescue party.
But all we hear is other
voices like our own, other bodies
tangled in the lines,
the repetition of a cry from every tree:

I can't help you, help me.

*ELEANOR WILNER*
*Vol. 4#1, 1979*

Days my tongue slips away.
I can't hold on to my tongue.
It's slippery like the lizard's tail
I try to grasp
but the lizard darts away.

મારી જીભ સરકી જાય છે.
*(mari jeebh sarki jai chay)*
I can't speak. I speak nothing.
Nothing. કાઈ નહિ, હું નથી બોલી શકતી
        *(kai nahi, hoo nathi boli shakti)*
I search for my tongue.

પરંતુ ક્યાં શોધું? ક્યાં?
*(parantu kya shodhu? Kya?)*

હું દોડતી દોડતી જાઉ છું:
*(hoo dhodti dhodti jaoo choo)*
But where should I start? Where?
I go running, running,

નદી કિનારે પહોંચી છું, નદી કિનારે.
*(nadi keenayray pohchee choo, nadi keenayray)*
reach the river's edge.
Silence એકદમ શાંત.
        *(akedum shant)*

નીચે પાણી નહિ, ઉપર પક્ષી નહિ.
*(neechay pani nahi, oopur pakshi nahi)*
Below, the riverbed is dry. Above,
the sky is empty: no clouds, no birds.
If there were leaves, or even grass
they would not stir today,
for there is no breeze.
If there were clouds
then, it might rain.

જો વાદળ હોત તો કદાચ વરસાદ આવે,
*(jo vadla hoat        toh kadach varsad aavay)*
જો વરસાદ પડે તો નદી પાછી આવે,
*(jo varsad puday toh nadi pachee aavay)*
જો નદી હોય, જો પાણી હોય, તો કદાચ લીલું લીલું દેખાય.

*(jo nadi hoy, jo pani hoy, toh kaeek leelu leelu daykhai)*
If the rains fell
then the river might return,
if the water rose again I might see something green
at first, then trees enough to fill a forest.
If there were some clouds that is.

જો વાદળા હોત તો.
*(jo vadla hoat toh)*
Since I have lost my tongue
I can only imagine
there is something crawling
beneath the rocks, now burrowing down
into the earth when I lift the rock.

જ્યારે પથ્થર ઉપાડુ.
*(jyaray patther oopadu)*
The rock is in my hand, and the dry
moss stuck on the rock
prickles my palm.
I let it drop
for I must find my tongue.
I know it can't be here
in this dry riverbed.
My tongue can only be
where there is water.

પાણી, પાણી,
*(pani, pani)*
ફૂ યાદ છે પેલી છોકરી.
*(hujoo yad chay paylee chokri)*
"ઠંડા પાણી, મીઠા પાણી," બોલતી બોલતી આવતી.
*("thunda pani, meetha pani," bolti bolti aavti)*
માથે કાળુ માટલુ, હાથમા પીત્તળનો પ્યાલો.
*(mathay kallu matlu, hathma pittulno pyalo)*
ઉભેલી ગાડી બાજુ આવતી.
*(oobhaylee gaadi baju aavti)*
બારી તરફ હાથ લંબાવીને પાણી આપતી.
*(bari taraf hath lumbaveenay pani aapti)*
અને હું, અતિશય તરસી,
*(unay hoo, ateeshay tarsi)*

મોટા મોટા ઘૂંટડા લેતી પી જતી.

(*mota mota ghuntada layti pee jati*)

ફ઼ુ યાદ છે પેલી છોકરી.

(*hujoo yad chay paylee chokri*)

Even water is scarce.
There was a little girl
who carried a black clay pitcher on her head,
who sold water at the train station.
She filled her brass cup with water,
stretched out her arm to me,
reached up to the window, up
to me leaning out the window from the train,
but I can't think of her in English.

II

You ask me what I mean
by saying I have lost my tongue.
I ask you, what would you do
if you had two tongues in your mouth,
and lost the first one, the mother tongue,
and could not really know the other,
the foreign tongue.
You could not use them both together
even if you thought that way.
And if you lived in a place where you had to
speak a foreign tongue,
your mother tongue would rot,
rot and die in your mouth
until you had to spit it out.
I thought I spit it out
but overnight while I dream,

મને હતુ કે આખ્યી જીભ આખ્ખી ભાષા,

(*munay hutoo kay aakhee jeebh aakhee bhasha*)

મેં થૂંકી નાખી છે.

(*may thoonky nakhi chay*)

પરંતુ રાત્રે સ્વપ્નામાં મારી ભાષા પાછી આવે છે.

(*parantoo rattray svupnama mari bhasha pachi aavay chay*)

ફૂલની જેમ મારી ભાષા મારી જીભ

(*foolnee jaim mari bhasha mari jeebh*)

મોઢામાં ખીલે છે.
*(modhama kheelay chay)*

ફુલની જેમ મારી ભાષા મારી જીભ
*(fulllnee jaim mari bhasha mari jeebh)*

મોઢામાં પાકે છે.
*(modhama pakay chay)*

it grows back, a stump of a shoot
grows longer, grows moist, grows strong veins,
it ties the other tongue in knots,
the bud opens, the bud opens in my mouth,
it pushes the other tongue aside.
Everytime I think I've forgotten,
I think I've lost the mother tongue,
it blossoms out of my mouth.
Days I try to think in English:
I look up, પેલો કાળો કાગડો
   *(paylo kallo kagdo)*

ઉડતો ઉડતો જાય, હુવે ઝાડે પહોંચે,
*(oodto oodto jai, huhvay jzaday pohchay)*

એની ચાંચમાં કાંઈક છે.—
*(ainee chanchma kaeek chay)*

the crow has something in his beak.
When I look up
I think: આકાશ, સુરજ
   *(aakash, suraj)*

and then: sky, sun.
Don't tell me it's the same, I know
better. To think of the sky
is to think of dark clouds bringing snow,
the first snow is always on Thanksgiving.
But to think: આકાશ, અસમાન, આભ.
   *(aakash, usman, aabh)*

માથે મોટા કાળા કાગડા ઉડે.
*(mathay mota kalla kagda ooday)*

કાગડાને માથે સુરજ, રોજે સુરજ.
*(kagdanay mathay suraj, rojjay suraj)*

એકપણ વાદળ નહિ, એટલે વરસાદ નહિ,
*(akepun vadul nahi, atelay varsad nahi)*

*એટલે અનાજ નહિ, એટલે રોટલી નહિ,*
(atelay anaj nahi, atelay rotli nahi)

*દાળ ભાત શાક નહિ, કાઇ નહિ, કૂછ બી નહિ,*
(dal bhat shak nahi, kai nahi, kooch bhi nahi)

*માત્ર કાગડા, કાળા કાગડા*
(matra kagda, kalla kagda)

Overhead, large black crows fly.
Over the crows, the sun, always
the sun, not a single cloud
which means no rain, which means no wheat,
no rice, no greens, no bread. Nothing.
Only crows, black crows.
And yet, the humid June air,
the stormiest sky in Connecticut
can never be *આકાશ*
        (aakash)

*ચોમાસામાં જ્યારે વરસાદ આવે*
(chomasama jyaray varsad aavay)

*આખી રાત આખો દે' વરસાદ પડે, વિજળી જાય,*
(aakhee raat aakho dee varsad puday, vijli jai)

*જ્યારે મા રસોડામાં ઘીને દીવે રોટલી વાંતી*
(jyaray ma rasodama gheenay deevay rotli vanti)

*શાક હલાવતી*
(shak halavti)

*રવિંદ્રસંગિત ગાતી ગાતી*
(Ravindrasangeet gaati gaati)

*સૌને બોલાવતી.*
(saonay bolavti)

the monsoon sky giving rain
all night, all day, lightning, the electricity goes out,
we light the cotton wicks in butter:
                candles in brass.
And my mother in the kitchen,
my mother singing:

*મોન મોર મેઘેર શુંગે, ઉડે ચોલે દિગ્દિગંતૈર પાને ...*
(mon mor megher shungay, ooday cholay dikdigontair panay)
I can't hear my mother in English.

III

In the middle of Maryland
you send me a tape recording
saying " કહ્ય આ અેક વાત તો કઇવીજ પડશે,
    *(huhvay aa ake vat toh kahveej padshay)*

અહેને બ્હાર કૂતરા ભસય, ભહળે ધોબી આવે,
*(bhalaynay bahr kootra bhasay, bhalay dhobi aavay)*

ભહળે શાકવાળી આવે, મારય આ વાત તો કઇવીજ પડશે.
*(bhalay shakvali aavay, maray aa vat toh kahveej padshay)*

ભહળે ટપાળી આવે, ભહળે કાગડા કૌ કૌ કરે,
*(bhalay tapali aavay, bhalay kagda kaw kaw karay)*

ભહળે રીક્શાનો અવાજ આવે,
*(bhalay rickshano avaj aavay)*

મારે તનય આ વાત તો કઇવીજ પડશે. "
*(maray tanay aa vat toh kahveej padshay)*
You talk to me,
    you say my name the way it should be said,
apologizing
for the dogs barking outside
for the laundryman knocking on the door,
apologizing because
the woman selling eggplants
is crying રીંગ્ણા, રીંગ્ણા door to door
      *(reengna, reengna)*
But do you know
how I miss that old woman, crying રીંગ્ણા, રીંગ્ણા.
        *(reengna, reengna)*
It's alright if the peddler's brass bells ring out,
I miss them too.
You talk louder, the mailman comes, knocking louder,
the crows caw-caw-cawing outside,
the rickshaw's motor put-put-puttering.
You say સુજુ બ્હેન કહ્ય તમારય માટય તબલા વગાડું છૂ.
    *(Suju bhen huhvay tamaray matay tabla vagadu choo)*
you say: listen to the tablas,
listen: ધા ધીન ધીન ધા    *(dha dhin dhin dha)*

ધા ધિન ધિન ધા  *(dha dhin dhin dha)*

listen ધા ધિન ધિન ધા  *(dha dhin dhin dha)*

ધિનક ધિનક ધિન ધિન  *(dhinaka dhinaka dhin dhin)*

ધિનક ધિનક ધિન ધિન  *(dhinaka dhinaka dhin dhin)*

ધા ધિન ધિન ધા  *(dha dhin dhin dha)*

ધિનક ધિનક ધિનક ધિનક  *(dhinaka dhinaka dhinaka dhinaka)*

ધા ધિન ધિન ધા  *(dha dhin dhin dha)*

ધિનક ધિનક ધિન ધિન  *(dhinaka dhinaka dhin dhin)*

I listen   I listen   I listen

ધા ધિન ધિન ધા  *(dha dhin dhin dha)*

I hear you   I hear you

ધિનક ધિનક ધિન ધિનક ધિનક ધિન ધિનક ધિનક ધિન

*(dhinaka dhinaka dhin dhinaka dhinaka dhin dhinaka dhinaka dhin)*

listen       listen       listen

Today I played your tape

over and over again

ધા ધિન ધિન ધા  *(dha dhin dhin dha)*

ધિનક ધિનક ધા  *(dhinaka dhinaka dha)*

I can't ધા *(dha)*

I can't ધા  *(dha)*

I can't forget    I can't forget

ધા ધિન ધિન ધા *(dha dhin dhin dha)*

*SUJATA BHATT*
*Vol. 5#2&3, 1980*

## NIÑA

*Niña, ven, a ver lo que traigo: caña, mangó,*
*leche condensada pa' hacerte un flan,*
*pan dulce con canela, mamey,*
*aguacate y mi tierra.*
I offer you this a part of *mi historia*,
something like *un mojo criollo*, a bit
of everything, a mosaic me.
*Caracoles salados pa' que oigas el mar,*
*pa' que te acompañe un azul caribe cielo.*

There's a beat I didn't tell you about
singing an undercurrent to my skin
strung tight against the bones
a sharp and strident sound and loud
you listen and hear my bongo bones.
Hey *nena*, laugh with me, hear that

shouting moaning wail
growing green and white gardenias
through the rich marrow soil
of my xylophone bones
my colorcoded *marimba* skin.
Dance this one with me

*que te saco a bailar*
give me *merengue, guaguancó,*
*crema de leche, besitos*
*de coco y madrugada* silhouetting
*las palmas* against the stray moon.
Hear this happiness, *mi nena tibia*

give me shouts like you want to yell
from the sewers and fire escapes
give me that dancing CubaRican beat
*y gritería en el rufo* summer nights

*con güiro, clave, maraca, bongó,*
*clave, maraca, bongó, bongó,*
*güiro, bongó, bongó, bongó.*
*Dale, mami, ven ven óyelo bien saborea*

that beat until your eyes see colors
blurring, you feel the sounds a dizzy
pounding gasping blur you feel you feel
you are the beat you blur you feel
you are it takes you it takes you
it makes you dance it makes you dance
it brings you home it stays it stays.

Befriend it, my friend, this is
that wild moonjazz beat, that beat
I didn't tell you about, hardly believing
you could hear. Oh listen, I believe you can.

*YOLANDA MANCILLA*
*Vol. 8#2, 1984*

# URBAN INDIANS, PIONEER SQUARE, SEATTLE

Walking the streets, we watch the people stare,
then quickly look away when they see us notice
them. It is not easy always being watched.
At times, we hunger to be invisible, to disappear
into the crowd the way a deer can disappear
in the brush and rest for half a day. We sit
on park benches and stay still as owls hiding
in barn rafters; once in a while we blink,
but one can barely see us breathe. We know
the tourists think we're drunks—we've been out
of work so long, eating in soup kitchens, sleeping
in missions—our clothes ragged; our shoes
are worn. Sometimes, we do find money
and drink, pretend to be happy—on good days
we remember how to laugh, and how, at fifteen,
we ran up the mountain behind home and watched
the eagles soar, feeling their power at the base
of our minds; those birds still move our thoughts
so high we get giddy at the mystery that runs
the world whenever we think of them. At times,
we think about returning home—there is no work
there, and relatives already have trouble making
ends meet, but at least there'd be cousins
to tease. Most of the time, we know such journeys
are impossible, to see us beaten like this would
make our loved ones cry. Here only strangers
see the pain that eats at us like acid eating
into the exposed surface on a metal plate,
and these strangers never see us anyway—
only their own visions of what they'll let us be.
It is better to be stared at than known when one has
so little left to give. We look after one another
when we can, and wonder, if the world don't
change soon, how much longer will any of us live.

*GAIL TREMBLAY*
*Vol. 8#2, 1984*

## GREAT INDIAN FATHER IN THE SUBWAY

Father rides the subway,
mutters to himself.
The rumble of subway swims
underground,
ignites his voice.

A beaver dam under the city:
flat tail warns of low sky.
Red clouds woven
like curved necks of geese
go into one hole,
come out another.

Great Father, Painted Horse,
sends smoke signals from
raised beaver mounds,
ancient hills where
his language rises to
completion
while the subway moves
speaking to itself like
an old man.

*DIANE GLANCY*
*Vol. 7#2, 1982*

# I REMEMBER HAIFA BEING LOVELY BUT

there were snakes in the
tent, my mother was
strong but she never
slept, was afraid of
dreaming. In Auschwitz
there was a numbness,
lull of just staying
alive. Her two babies
gassed before her, Dr.
Mengele, you know who
he is? She kept her
young sister alive
only to have her die
in her arms the night
of liberation. My mother
is big boned, but she
weighed under 80 lbs
It was hot, I thought
the snakes lovely. No
drugs in Israel, no
food. I got pneumonia,
my mother knocked the
doctor to the floor
when they refused,
said I lost two in
the camp and if this
one dies I'll kill
myself in front of
you. I thought that
once you became a
mother, blue numbers
appeared mysteriously,
tattooed on your arm

*LYN LIFSHIN*
*Vol. 8#1, 1983*

# TAMSEN DONNER AT ALDER CREEK

*Tamsen Donner, botanist, teacher, mother of*
*three children and wife of George Donner, the*
*leader of the Donner Party, chose to stay with*
*her dying husband near Donner Lake instead of*
*accompanying her young daughters to safety in*
*California.*

It began with certain choices:
the rescue party waited
while you muffled your silent girls
in wool—
    Georgia    Eliza    Frances
    you taught them to recite
    their little history in California:
    *We are the children*
    *of Mr. and Mrs. George Donner*
    *and our parents are dead.*
Then the storm clouds bellied down,
and single-file your children moved
across the frozen lake,
a cord that
   tugged
      and tugged.

You pulled in an opposite direction,
back to Alder Creek
through drifts up to your armpits
    (some say you walked 14 miles
    in the time a strong man
    could walk 5).
On the way the snow
turned unexpectedly to meadow—
    wild tulip, lupine,
    larkspur, creeping hollyhock
teasing your numb feet.
You thought you were back in the Platte Valley
working in your sketchbook.
You hallucinated birds.

That green world came
to Alder Creek with you
and for three days you were framed
by the flat    Illinois pasture
where your husband first saw you
sketching plants.
Together you watched the spring
break sharp and green
through 15 feet of snow.
Later when the fever
made him rage and burn
you held your hands up to his face
as to the sun.

Today the snow is back.
You have bound
your husband's wasted body
in a sheet.
Now no one touches you
     no child    no man
nothing is extraneous
to your hardened purpose:
everything is honed away
by ice.
This morning
you are so light
your footprints barely
mark the snow.
Your bones are tools
and you are free to write
the history of starvation,
the text of love,
the language of
     wild tulip
     lupine
     larkspur
a design beneath the snow.

*MAREAN L. JORDAN*
*Vol. 7#2, 1982*

# OCTOBER LIGHT

Dying leaves
spill like blood across
the grass. Women gather dried
bouquets of seed pods,
bizarre grey bells
clinging to barren limbs.

Voices of our mothers' friends
climb the wind like chaff.

In the houses we grew up in
women sit and talk. Cups
of leftover coffee
warm their hands. They speak
with onion-skin whispers
of a remembered discontent.
Regret, sprinkled like salt,
preserves their pain.

Conversations with our mothers
catch the wind and spin.

Orange mornings when withered
leaves fall like death's shadow
all golden on the ground
we sit inside and talk.
Smoke and old wives' fears
stain our fingers with yellow
nicotine. Cats' paws snag
our breath. Outside, the wind.

*BARBARA BALDWIN*
*Vol. 2#2, 1977*

## SESTINA, WINCHELL'S DONUT HOUSE

Watching the black hours through to morning,
I'd set out each successive tray of grease-
cooked donuts on the rack, chocolate and pink-
frosted, to harden beneath the fluorescent light,
talk to crazy Harry, count the change,
listen to top-forty radio. Mostly, I was alone.

Every stranger's suspect when you're alone.
A woman was beaten badly early one morning
by a man who sneaked in the back while she made change,
so I'd rehearse scenarios of scooping grease,
flinging it at the assailant's face, cooking the light
or dark flesh to curl away at the impact, angry pink.

The cab drivers came in every night, faces polished pink
and boyish, arriving in pairs or alone.
Their cabs clotted like moths at the building's light.
They were outlaws and brothers, despised men who rise in the morning.
They'd swagger, still dapper if fattened on sweets and grease,
call me sugar and honey. I smiled. I kept the change.

Often I was too busy to see the darkness change,
flush from black to blue to early pink.
At four o'clock, my face smeared with grease,
I think I was happiest, although most alone.
The harder hours were those of fullblown morning,
fighting depression, sleeping alone in the light.

Linda came in at six, awash with light,
businesslike, making sure there'd be enough change
to get her through the rigors of the morning.
She had a hundred uniforms; I remember pink.
Sometimes she'd cheat, leave me to work alone,
sneak out to flirt in parked cars, fleeing lifetimes of grease.

I can see her cranking the hopper, measuring grease,
indefatigable, wired on coffee, just stopping to light
her cigarettes. She didn't want to be alone.
It was only my fantasy that she could change,
stop wearing that silly, becoming pink,
burn free of the accidents, husband and children, some morning.

I remember walking home those mornings, smelling of grease,
amazed in summer's most delicate pink early light,
to shower, change, and sleep out the hot day alone.

*JAN CLAUSEN*
*Vol. 3#1, 1978*

# EARTH PLACE

*(for Mary Simmons)*

Listen
to the voices
push and fall
then open
eyes to the brown
afternoon

Together
we slide
down the Indian bronze
of your forehead
old woman
wet field
furrows
woman

and a fast
dance
in the changing season
changing woman
housebound
through winter
and we fly
on star quilts

our ship spinning
inward
our pilot
Coyote
between this earth
and her moon

*WENDY ROSE*
*Vol. 8#2, 1984*

## WOMEN OF SALT

Whether we reach or stoop,
salt weighs down our veins
until it works through skin

to collect on the upper lip
where our slow tongues take
it in again. If we hold out

our bare arms to the orphan
calf, his blue tongue will wrap
the wrist tight as a washrag.
And if we stand naked all night

in the woods without blinking,
the deer don't tense or hide
from us. Licking, they gather
to glean salt till our spines

surface, our jawbones shine. Lips
blur and breasts melt away, a frame
of teeth and hair is left behind.

And every time we grieve we make
sounds that say we're homing
back down to that bed of salt

and gills, soft place where
we were hooked before we knew a name
for thirst or a way to swallow tears.

*SHEILA DEMETRE*
*Vol. 5#1, 1980*

## WEED

She stood, a weed tall in the sun.
She grew like that and went
over it again and again trying to be tall
trying not to die in the drying sun
the seeming turbulence of waiting
the sun so yellow
so still

There was nothing else to do. It was like that
in her day, and the sun who rose so bright
so full of fire reminded her of that.
It was the sun that did it; it was the rain.
She stood it all, and more:
the water pounding from the high rock face
of the mesas that made her yard
she knew where she was growing. Didn't
she know what sun will do, what happens to weeds
when their growing time's done? Didn't she care?
She got the sun into her, though.
The fire. She drank the rain for fuel.
She stood there in the day, growing,
trying to stand tall like a right weed would.

The drying was part of it.
The dying. Come from heat, the transformation
of fire. The rain helped because it understood
why she just stood there, growing,
tall in the heat and bright.

*PAULA GUNN ALLEN*
*Vol. 8#2, 1984*

# ON ARRIVING AT LING-NAN, JANUARY, 1949

*Two tz'u to the tune of Lin-chiang Hsien*
*"The Immortal by the River"*

1.

Ten years gone.
    I am still the same.
The dust of the battlefield
    is all I see.
Was anything left behind
    in the ash?
A manor can hold its dreams forever
But in this dull cold
    the strings would wail.

Sunrise over parks
    of blooming peach trees:
Someone walked here
    with me once.
Spring winds fill
    and freshen my face.
All that is now the past:
A noise
    chasing the Ch'in-huai River.

2.

North to south I travel.
    How far have I come?
Dark clouds cover
    the mountain range.
Below, the soil is warm.
I'll stay a while.
When I am lonely,
    I pick lonely flowers.
When I drink just a bit,
    I stay awake longer.

At sky's end, tiny waves
    split the sea.
The tide comes in
    and the world is blue.
Don't ask the past
    where you are going.
Lakes and mountains
    frightened my dreams last night.
Now wind and rain move me
    closer to all people.

*LI CHI*
translated by *LI CHI*
and *MICHAEL O'CONNOR*
*Vol. 5#2&3, 1980*

The river is where we go sometimes. When the air is wet, it rains. When there is more, that makes the river. Sometimes clouds. If they lose a part, my mother says seagull.

Colors have names. Seagull is a cloud that sleeps on the river. White is seagull, cloud. The colors all have names.

My father goes in a boat. He comes back. The boat goes under the water, he says. We stand by the river. He is down beside me and loosens a rock and throws it. "Like that," he says. A seagull goes screaming there to look. "Then we come back up."

The rock is hidden. I cannot find the color.

. . .

I am taken places. There is school now. She is tall and plays the piano. I said my name and my favorite color was red. She showed me to draw the letters.

My brother takes me to a movie. I could not hold the money. He is eight.

Then that time I thought it would be a movie, but we went in a car, our family, all four. My brother said he could make a boat. My mother wore a dress. We saw my father's water and his boat. It is gray and shaped like a seagull sleeping on the water. It had gray colors inside.

We got on. I wore new shoes and they made noise like my brother and I jumping up and down. We jump on the couch. Everything for the boat was gray with some red. It smelled like the river. That was green, and some brown like under the porch. The gray spot on the floor of the garage, too.

My brother saw the periscope. I saw clocks with numbers wrong. They had only the little hands, red, and they did not go around. They shivered like the little leaves on the Christmas tree. I could touch cold steel. Then my hand smelled like it.

We went down round ladders. My mother pushed down her dress, but wind came and picked it up. My father laughed. I had on overalls.

There are men here. Some are white, some are brown, some are yellow. The brown ones are called colored. My father told me once at a store.

The men are afraid of my father. They are afraid of me. It is a small place, down in here, after the stairs. It is hot, but all the steel is cold. The men call my father Sir, but his first name is Jake. When we go back up the stairs my mother holds her dress better.

Sometimes when I eat I pretend I can be the food, falling all the way down to my stomach. After the boat I felt like I have been in a gray stomach. I can still smell it on my hands in the car.

. . .

He wears a uniform. It is one color except for ribbons. The ribbons are striped and shiny with green, red, white, yellow going up and down. Once when his coat was on a chair, I looked in back of them. I thought there would be something else there.

They have gold colored pins in back, like the one my aunt sent me for Christmas. My mother keeps it so I don't stick myself.

The ribbons are for places he went in a war. At the movies we saw pictures of it. War pictures are black and white with a crackly gray voice talking over. Ships slept on the water, then smoke.

Maps are colored like the ribbons. Yellow states, red ones, green Connecticut. I live in Connecticut. Blue lines are rivers and all blue for oceans. The tops of mountains are white because of snow.

I got tired looking at the ribbons. The movie pictures of war are black and white, but ribbons are colors. They are flat. The world in school by the blackboard is round. It turns. Usually when I close my eyes and spin the world, then I point and look, I land in water. My brother laughs. He can swim.

Water is blue. I look for blue but there is no blue stripe on the ribbons. No crackly gray like the talking voice at the movie. There are gold pins holding them, no smoke back there. But he says they are for places he went in a war.

. . .

His uniform is navy blue. That is black, but not really. I thought it was at first. He held it in the light and showed me I was wrong.

I looked in the old book about colors—red apple, yellow flower, green tree, blue sky. The black hat in the book could be navy blue. But the word says black.

His uniform is navy blue, they said. I ask about the hat. The hat is navy blue. "If I forgot my hat, I would not be in uniform."

I say the sky is blue, but he says not always. Not really either. "It has no real color," he says. "The dust in the air makes it look blue."

I look for blue dust. He finds gray dust on his uniform and rubs it off. I ask why can't I see the dust in the air.

"It's there. It's too small to see." I am afraid for a while. Then I learn to see dust in the sunlight, only not the blue kind.

Then I forgot my book on the table. It got dust, but no new colors on top. I think dust might be like water, clear in a glass, blue in the ocean. I am happy.

Days go by, blue like dust, gray like dust. Everything is all right so I ask about water. They say it has no color. I was right.

. . .

In the summer he wears a white uniform. Still the ribbons are on it. In the summer I go swimming. The water is blue.

I ask again about water. It is clear, they say. It has no color.

"Is it white then?"

No, white is not a color. White is the empty place where there is no color. In my book, a cloud is white. Snow is white. Snow White had lips as red as rubies. A hat is black.

Black, they say, is all colors mixed together. I do it at school, spreading wet paints until they go past navy blue.

Wash my hands off in colorless water. Black is all colors mixed together. White is no color. They are opposites. The uniforms for summer and winter are opposites. The ribbons are the same, gold pin in the back.

. . .

Water has no color and no taste. Paper is white, but tastes like dust. And old chewing gum. I put off spitting it out. Then it tastes like a scab.

Black can taste like licorice. Before I wash my hands I tasted black. It was salty in finger paint. The teacher took a brown paper towel, wet it and scrubbed my face. A brown paper towel is really khaki, another uniform.

Khaki is almost flesh, not quite. In my book the baby is flesh colored. A crayon is marked FLESH. I use it, but I cannot draw a baby. Mine is too thin.

Some of the men on the ship were khaki. Some were BURNT SIENNA. I broke the BURNT SIENNA drawing a tree trunk. When I put it back in the box, it looked like the rainbow had a tooth missing.

. . .

Once we went, all four, in another boat. It was on the river and we took a picnic. We rented a rowboat, which was painted gray but had a khaki smell. We rolled along the water, my father moving the oars.

Green river, burnt sienna trees, yellow flowers, blue sky. The wind was pink, then it turned yellow. First we stopped and had our picnic, even with a white tablecloth on a grassy place.

Then it was time to go. The wind had been turning yellow, and then it felt green. In the boat going back, he rowed and was angry.

Then we lost part of the sky. First blue fell asleep to gray, then the clouds floated and landed some birds on top of the trees. Green trees turned gray, then their trunks were lost. Then the mud brown riverbank was gone and we were lost. The cloud came close to us like dust, or shadow and cave and a mouth closing. We were inside of a stomach.

We are inside of my father's boat then, and he is angry. I can tell because the oars sound like his footsteps on the ladder. The fog makes us seem like inside of a television set. The sound is turned down. The air tickles like spider webs, and somewhere far, animals are moaning.

My brother says he thinks he sees the dock. We rented the boat at a dock. My father rows where my brother says, but then he has to push away from a tree log with the oar. He pushes, whack. Tree fingers scrape their nails around the boat.

I think I cried. He is angry now. Are we lost. I want to know. He says no, stop it. She holds me but her dress is damp. I hear her heart inside her body, and she sounds afraid.

He makes the oars slap the water, snap, slap, like cap guns. We are not lost, he says. We will be at the dock in a minute. We could be there sooner, but my brother told him the wrong way to go.

Then we went on, going more, slap, snap. Moaning near us. I may have become fog somewhere. I was afraid for my colors. They would not come back. I was bad and gray punished. But then gray must have been sorry. Colors came back.

. . .

Maybe a year went by. Summer sifted sunny days and dust. Winter sifted snow and sleeping. My brother was ten. I remember because he got in trouble at school. His homework always got scribbled with drawings of planes and ships on the water. The ships had flags of flames going up, and smoke.

Then one night my father got home late and dinner was almost cold. He set his briefcase by the door. He hung his uniform jacket on the back of his dinner chair.

My mother said bless. We had meat with gravy to go on it. We had white baked potatoes freckled with pepper. We did not talk. When my brother was in trouble at school we ate inside a fog of no noise. I remember the colors. My father's jacket hung on the back of the chair. There were ribbons on it. No one spoke. Forks tinked on china, sharp like bright stripes on dark navy blue.

My brother liked to look at the jacket. He was in trouble at school then, but he did not cry. Not anymore. Boys aren't supposed to. But he kept looking at the jacket.

Maybe he wanted to find out if my father was mad at him. When he is angry, my father's voice has a color that has no name. My brother asked a question to try to hear it.

"In the war, how many planes did you shoot down?"

My father put down his fork. The butter in my potato was golden, but I could not taste it.

"I personally did not shoot anyone. I was part of a crew." My father moved his tongue around his lips. "It's not like baseball, where you get your batting average."

He picked up his fork and took a bite of potato. "It's like tug-'o-war. The whole team pulls."

My brother's voice wanted to cry, but he told a lie instead. "It's for my homework." How many, he wanted to know. "When it's over, don't they tell you something like how many were yours?"

My mother finishes putting gravy on her meat. She slaps the ladle into the gravy boat. Three brown spots come to the white tablecloth, going yellow and clear at the edges.

My father says to stop asking questions. "This is not a topic for the dinner table." His voice does not want to cry.

I was afraid then. But I had to know how he felt. I was afraid to see his eyes. I looked as high as I dared. His lips were the color of dust.

*CAROL ORLOCK*
*Vol. 7#3, 1983*

# ANOTHER PART OF THE COUNTRY

*LAUREL RUST*

*for A.W.K.*

*I've worked in nursing homes as a nurses' aide for many years and this piece is about one woman, Amy, whom I was privileged to know. I'd like to dedicate it to her with her full name, but I don't know where her family is or the legal implications. As it is, I have changed her first name a little.*

*Nursing homes are unique worlds, and I had trouble deciding how much of that context to include. My main intent was and is to share Amy with others, preserve some of her life. I asked her if she would allow me to do this and she was pleased. Originally I included only her words and not my own feelings and reactions towards her, but because one myth of the institutionalized, "senile" elderly is that they are not responsive to "reality," I included my presence to show how intimately she was. Much of the confusion, withdrawal, hostility, repeated phrases, etc., that are considered symptoms of "senility" are more accurately a reaction to an environment where seldom does anyone speak with them or listen to them or be with them in any kind of genuine, egalitarian manner: the literature on aging supports this as do my own experiences.*

*I feel that in feminist circles, when the subject of women and aging comes up, nursing home women, especially those who cannot or do not communicate or relate to "reality" as we do, are very often forgotten despite all the adulation of hags and crones. I get angry when others refer to nurses' aide work in nursing homes as shit work: the pay is certainly shit, but coming to know these women is like nothing else.*

In Amy's room in the nursing home there are three identical narrow beds with metal rails, three small closets all in a row, three hospital tables, three small metal bedside cabinets, and three plastic water pitchers with three plastic glasses.

Amy's bed is closest to the door, which is only closed when someone has died. Next to her is Isabel, who repeats "lebalebalebaleba" with varying inflections and occasionally says a sentence, such as "I want to go home," and looks at you, amazed. "Lebalebalebaleba" resumes at fever pitch, her face tight with concentration, her thin hands patting her thin thighs, her bony chest. In the bed next to the window is Molly with her thick shock of white hair and her big, square face. When you feed her or turn her or dress her, Molly roars. Mostly she is in bed, moving her hands in front of her face and watching them. Outside the window is the big concrete parking lot.

Amy is "ambulatory" and one of the very few here who are labeled "self care." This means she can feed herself when the tray arrives three times a day. She can take herself to the bathroom. Unlike the others, most of whom are "heavy care" and nearly all of whom are women, Amy will not be spoon fed, not be tied in a wheelchair, not be changed and turned every two hours night and day, not be put to bed after lunch and remain there until morning. Within the institution's rigid schedule, Amy has some small choices because she can walk, see, hear, and talk. But like the sixty or so others, Amy has to take the medicine she is prescribed, which in her case includes mind-altering drugs. Her body is handled as though it is no longer hers. She has to stay in her bed all night; if she tries to climb out, she will be "restrained," which means tied into the bed until morning. She is not allowed into the kitchen. She is not allowed to leave the building.

Amy is awakened at 7 a.m. every morning, rolled up in bed with a tray on the table over her lap. An aide will hand her clothes to wear. By mid-morning, Amy will have modified her attire, perhaps adding another shirt, rolling up her pants, tying a scarf around her neck, putting on her coat. Throughout the day she may join the others lined up in the activities room where the television is always on. She will be allowed to range the halls with their fluorescent lights and linoleum floors; with women in wheelchairs, geri chairs, walkers; with rushing aides, laundry carts, medicine carts, and the loudspeaker with its constant commands: "Mary, Hannah needs assistance in the dining room," which means Hannah has wet her pants.

There is no space which is entirely Amy's own. Not even her self. Every two hours at night the light in her room will be switched on while Isabel and Molly are changed and turned, while the aides feel Amy's linen beneath her hips to be sure it is dry. Noise and light come in through the open door, which Amy is not allowed to close. Amy is allowed what personal possessions can fit into her tiny space, but if she has photographs or vases or nearly anything, chances are they will eventually be lost, broken, ruined in various ways. Any jewelry of value will be kept locked at the nurses' desk. If she gets any mail, it may or may not be read to her.

Amy's diagnosis is senile dementia. She is considered crazy. She talks non-stop, her face focused, animated, and attentive. Her expressiveness is considered insanity; her way of seeing, senility; her aging as an invasion, a rotting. Her life is considered to be over and because of this she is not perceived or treated as creative, adaptive, engaged—all the attributes of being human and alive. Instead, she barely exists in a limbo of invisibility where her body, her self, and her expression are not considered her own. She is entertaining to the staff not because she has a lively sense of humor and a quick mind that is sensitive to what is going on around her, but because she is crazy and everything she says is nonsense, because she does not know what she is saying.

Because Amy is ambulatory and self-care, she has certain advantages. But like the other women here, she is talked to and talked about and treated as though she were a child, a "cute little old lady," a deviant, a delinquent. Often she is talked about in her presence in the third person as though she is not here at all.

When I first began working here, one of the staff told me that "Amy is off the deep end." But where is the final edge in a place like this with its monotonous hallways, its identical beds, its artificial and unnatural oblivion? What is this if not a deep end?

Over the months I came to know Amy's ways well. I came to know her well enough to feel at times that I could follow her, to feel in moments that we understood something of each other. Her past remained largely inaccessible to me: her "records" include nothing of her experiences other than marital status and medical history, and because I am an aide I am not allowed access to them. If I were, it would be an invasion of her privacy, yet the nurses and administrators are free to say Amy is crazy in anyone's hearing. If they suspect she masturbates, everyone will know.

What I know of her past is that she'd been raised in Utah, that her father was a doctor, that she had asthma as a child, that she had been a dancer, that she was widowed and had two children. I write this as a record of one woman's creative struggle to exist in the world of an institution that regards her as a non-entity, where upon moving in a stranger to her will sit beside her for ten minutes and ask questions like "who is the president?" in order to ascertain Amy's "orientation to reality." According to her records, Amy exhibits none.

Amy ranges the halls all day wearing her own combination of clothes. Her body is very thin and slightly stooped, and she moves lightly as though floating. Her long thinning hair is tied up with a bright scarf: this is something she takes pleasure in doing every morning, coiling her hair on top of her head with her long arms as she sits on the edge of the bed. Her aqua eyes are deep and large, her bony cheeks red and her skin that light brown shade one often sees in very old white people. She talks nearly non-stop in a seemingly incoherent manner, nodding and often answering herself with "uh-*huh*, uh-*huh* dearie." All the while her face is animated with emotions, her eyes gazing directly into yours. She stops and chats with anyone, sometimes patting them or holding their hand, smiling. "Remember to laugh when you go around corners." Sometimes her rapid talk is filled with fury. "No sir, it's this one and that one and that one, uh-huh, and if I say yes they say well that's too bad. And if I stop talking I'll just stop." The staff laughs and smiles at crazy Amy who can talk circles around your head.

Amy keeps carefully rolled up pieces of toilet paper in her stuffed purse. They are tied neatly with shreds of toilet paper. Often she has one in her hand. She calls them her "little ones." She keeps them under her pillow, in her drawer, in her bed, until the housekeeper comes through and cleans things up, throws the little ones away and rearranges everything according to institutional order.

One day I made a little one and handed it to her.

"Here's another little one," I said.

"Well my my," she said, taking it, "you certainly cracked me." She laughed and made a face. "You certainly saw into that one, you blew the whistle on that little story."

Talking is Amy's way of knowing she is still alive. It is her intense, continuous engagement. It is one of the very means of creative expression allowed her. It is a way of creatively adapting to a monotonous and inhuman environment where no one really talks with her. If she stops talking, she'll "just stop." It's not so much death the very old fear as losing awareness of existence. It's our own fear of death, those of us who have the knowledge of a lesser number of years in the cells of our bodies and our consciousness, that often makes us oblivious to all the awareness in the old and makes it alien to us not because of any truth in the myth that the elderly are diminished, reduced to bare bones, but because it is so radically different and so unique to each individual.

Amy has a wonderful way of saying things. I often think of my grandmother, whose "hallucinatory" talk aptly described the undercurrents in my family that no one would talk about or admit. Like all of us, the very old have codes of their own: sometimes you can find your way into them and sometimes you can't. I struggled with the question of if I was intruding. Does an 83-year-old woman want to be comprehensible? Does she want me to follow her? How does one see and feel the world after living for 83 years? Working with the very old, one learns new ways of speaking, of listening, of communicating; new ways of seeing. Often the exchange is startlingly immediate and direct, a gut-level communication that transgresses the boundaries established by social conventions. Many of the very old have no use for such conventions.

Amy and I have developed an intimacy that is hard to describe, an intimacy that makes me think of companionship differently because Amy does not know my name and has never asked. We sit and simply take up talking, wherever and whenever we are. Talking with Amy who "exhibits no orientation to reality" is a wonderful experience in which we are always in the present, and the present could be anything we choose to create between us.

I asked Amy one day if I could interview her. She had been sick in bed for a couple of days. I wanted to be able to write down things she said. My pencil, though, couldn't keep up with her pace.

Amy was propped up in her bed, surrounded by her little ones, the crown of her head encircled with a tightly rolled bright pink scarf. She looked down at her long, bony legs stretched out straight in front of her and said, "My, it feels funny, it isn't mine anymore."

I asked her what it is like to age.

"I could tell it in one fell swoop, it is H-E-double L. It is because I am used to having my own way and when I see all of this and see I'm fifty and sixty and seventy years older than they are and I'm still not pushing through, doing nothing, monotonous—I say to my family, 'I'm just going to be here for this little time. Don't stop here with me, go on with yours.'

"It's not very nice when you think of what it used to be, what a beautiful thing it was, all of us running here and there. Beautiful. I've had a lovely, lovely living, myself, growing old, shabby, aging. When I get this far I have to look myself in the eye and say uh-*huh*, dearie, this is as far as you go: I have to think of myself.

"When I could dance I was happy. I used to dance on the stage in Salt Lake City and Europe and places everyone came. I could dance and I could count and I can still count, but this is too much for it. You girls are the ones keeping it going. If we didn't have you we wouldn't have a chance. You do things beautifully, you do things differently and carefully and there's a shine to it and don't you forget that."

I asked her what she thought about death.

"Oh I'm past that too. So many of them, I'm the oldest one of them in this creative thing. They're all crazy to be counted, and here I can take one look at it, read it up and down, know it from A to Z, but even with that I have to sit up to breathe and I have to be careful.

"But only the little ones can see it quicker than you. Some of the little ones can lead you better, because they don't feel things like you do."

I asked her if her consciousness had changed with age.

"Oh my yes," she laughed, "but the main things don't get thrown over. I just chow-chow-chow because it makes you feel more relieved not to take in too much. But it's wonderful when there's another voice in here."

"How do you like living here?"

"Well let me think how to say it. None of us had much in common. Oh I don't think I'd like it. It's too satisfied, it all has to be done on cue. They just leave everyone in here. As soon as you walked in and said hello, they'd say hello, and you could see how it would be, because you can't wait on them and they can't wait on you. Oh yes I'd rather be home. You see I'm spoiled to death. I had one brother and then another, I'd run up and down, but now"—she starts to cough—"I'm wishing I'd just stayed still. And not make my eyes move. Just close them quietly."

Over the next few days Amy grew increasingly weak and stayed in bed, her hands clenched, listless and quiet. I arrived one day to find her nowhere around: she'd been taken to the hospital, found to have pneumonia. I was afraid she was going to die, I'd seen it happen so often. I always feared coming to work, filling my laundry cart and starting down the halls, room by room, and finding a bed empty, stripped, a plastic garbage bag on the mattress filled with possessions for the family to retrieve. After work I drove to the hospital.

Amy turned and looked at me when I walked in. There was an oxygen tube in each nostril that looped around her ears and came together again at that place in her throat where in self-defense classes I'd been taught you could kill an attacker with your finger. Her fine-boned hands, the veins raised as cords, were clenched into fists and her breathing was shallow as that of a newborn bird. She took my hand into hers and smiled weakly. I realized that I had worried that she wouldn't recognize me in a different environment from that in which she knew me. I realized seeing her in a place other than the nursing home made me a little uneasy.

The shades on the other side of the room were open and we could see the mountains.

"It's beautiful outside today," I said, "I could even see Mt. Baker from the bridge."

"Well I'm glad you found a place for yourself," she said. "I hope you do it justice."

"How are you feeling?"

"Oh I'm not doing anything, lazy."

"How was your ambulance ride?"

"Oh it was wonderful being in the wild wide open. I've always loved that." She looked at the woman in the next bed. "I wonder how she feels, my little friend Virginia. I came over here to take care of her and then I fell down.

"Oh they don't leave you alone in here. They're always in and out. I was crashing in and out and couldn't get around this thing," she said, gesturing to her chest, "and dad said everything was fine. Everyone's been calling me but I'm too tired to chat and chat with all of them. But I'm glad you're here, I'll always remember that."

Amy tried to keep looking in my direction but her head would fall back and soon she would be turned toward the window where dusk was falling. The room was full of her struggle to breathe. Both of us were quiet, holding hands. She squeezed my hand from time to time as though to comfort me.

"I want to find my family and tell them I'm going over to see dad and where they all are. I just want this all to be over with. Why don't we just blow the whistle and all go home?

"I'm standing on a street corner looking up and down for somebody. I haven't seen anybody for quite a while.

"It's just too much, too fast."

Seeing Amy struggling for breath, fidgeting with her chest as though to free herself, so frail and quiet, her eyes gazing in an agitated way around the room, I started to cry. She looked down at our hands together on the sheet and said quietly, "I think this is all filled up. If we could just wait until Thanksgiving and start all over and have another big one like this."

The nurse came in and tried to give Amy her medicine.

"Come on," she said cheerfully, "let's be good and take our medicine so we feel better."

Amy looked up at her and said in the chatty style I'd seen her use so often in the nursing home, "Oh I'm busy with all the youngsters." She smiled but she wouldn't open her mouth. Finally the nurse had to force the medicine down her. As soon as she was out of the room, Amy spit it out and wiped her mouth.

"It's ridiculous," she said fiercely, "it's wasted. I don't want anything like this."

When I left that night, I told her to sleep well.

"Oh I'm saving sleep for when it is really over," she said.

I visited Amy nearly every day in the weeks she was in the hospital. Back in the nursing home they weren't sure if they should save her bed or not. The housekeeper had already steam cleaned it.

In the hospital Amy wouldn't eat, saying she was "full of goobly-gook from here to here, there just isn't any place left." She was given IVs, which she ripped out. Her hands were loosely restrained and she still managed to pull out the IVs. Yet she was pale and extremely weak, and referred frequently and in oblique but clear ways to the question of whether she should fight for her life or "close my eyes quietly," and if it was even right to wish for all of it to end. She was taken off oxygen. She moaned in pain often, turning away from me when she did. She continued to spit out her medicine. Her lips were chapped and I rubbed balm into them; she opened her lips and let me. I'd bring her coffee and ice cream and she'd eat a little and talk about picnics in the country, about driving the old car full speed on the back roads.

"But it's just too fast, too sudden and too much. I wish it would all slow down.

It's so quiet in here I feel scared sometimes. I just have to keep talking to keep myself from going to pieces.

"And when it was my husband and he was gone, it wasn't anything like this, it was so sudden, like a great rift. You just didn't know what to do, whether to see people or if you should say anything at all."

She looked at the t.v. her roommate was watching with the volume off.

"It's boring, all those people with their mouths open.

"I've been wanting to get ahold of my father, he always carried me through. It's ridiculous, all this, it all means *father*.

"It's so quiet in here. I don't hear the voices from down below.

"I ache all over. I just want everything to stop."

I asked her if I brought strawberries and peaches, would she eat with me?

"Oh that would be beautiful. I've always lived off that. But you might go your way and I another. We'll just have to keep our fingers crossed. I just don't know what to plan for; it all goes back to the dark ages."

*I dreamt one night that I was driving my old sky-blue Valiant down a hot, dusty dirt road that was still under construction, down a long hill to a ferry dock in a small green harbor. The ferry had just left. I noticed the wake on the water and that it was dusk. Amy was sitting beside me, wordlessly, looking. I slowed down because I knew there wouldn't be another ferry for a while.*

I took her a bouquet of daffodils and she stuck her whole face into them.

"Oh it's a crazy, crazy old world. It used to be so good and now it's slowly stopping and everyone is rushing here and there. Who would have thought I'd end up like this, an old lady. I just want all this back and forth to get over and be on the outside. But when I move just my little toe I ache all over.

"I'm afraid to sleep at night. They come in and go out. I just don't like all this coming down and landing, it just burns all through me."

She looked down at our clasped hands.

"It helps having something to hold. I'm such a coward. I was afraid it would be like this. If only we could fall back and sleep, and then it would be all over, just the two of us.

"It must be horrible for you, a young girl listening to me moaning. But it's nice to have somebody hear it. And if I'm not here when you come back, I'll leave a note on this door and that one.

"Tell me, what comes after the afternoon?"

As I left that evening, I heard her say quietly as I walked out the door and she lay gazing at the ceiling, "Hold on to me. Hold on to me."

I arrived just as she had ripped out her IVs again. Her hands had become black and blue. She was furious, talking non-stop as the nurse put in a new one, and in the middle of her furious speech I heard her say "and I'm tired of people who come by just to be nice and say hello, goodbye."

She drank a few swallows of the coffee I'd brought her. The energy of her anger made me feel she was getting stronger.

"I'm sick of being hovered over, pricked and jabbed. I just don't care anymore."

"Amy," I said, "do you think I come here just to be nice?"

"Well I think maybe you do, because I've seen you doing things you don't really want to do. But you don't know what this means to me."

I told her if she kept ripping out her IVs she'd starve to death. I said she probably knew that. I said starvation was a painful, slow way to die.

We talked about death a little: or I did. I asked her if she minded me talking like this, and she nodded quietly that she didn't mind. I told her the things I thought about it, the deaths I'd seen, near death experiences I'd read about, the light around Stanley's body when he died.

Sometimes she seemed to want to die and sometimes she didn't. What was hard was all the "crashing in and out," the "coming down and landing," the constant exhausting pain. What was also hard was daily being invaded, "hovered over," the daily things around her, as important to her as the possibility of death and "what to plan for." I found I had to remind myself of this.

I remembered how in the nursing home if I managed to leave her tray in her room long after the trays were supposed to be picked up, that within a few hours she would have cleaned her plate. She liked to take her time with things, she liked to do things "carefully" and "with a shine to them." And I realized she didn't need me to translate her, to drive her to the ferry dock, though I felt as I talked about death that she was willing me to talk. When I left, I told the nurse to try leaving her alone with her tray. It worked. The nurse said, "It's so hard with these old people, they don't tell us anything about them."

But I drove home wondering if Amy trusted me, if I was another intrusion, some kind of macabre voyeur. She was right: I often do what I do not want to do. She'd blown the whistle on my little story. But not this, not seeing her, not coming to know her. I began to see the ways in which I needed her. And the next day, the drift of her conversation made me feel she'd read my mind, that she'd been in the car beside me on the dusty road still under construction.

The inflection of her voice was a combination of anger and tenderness.

"There's nothing here that can conclude with anything. This is a children's rendezvous, just an ordinary thing, just a little chit-chat. I like things that I can chat about, that I don't exactly have to know what I am thinking. I'm too old to start in and think about it all, know what I think and what I want. My homecoming is entirely different from this place and I'm years and years older than you girls."

"Amy, are you talking in part about our friendship?"

"Well there's nothing here that has stirred me to the limits of anything. I just don't think there's enough of anything in me; I can't believe in it. It's just a question of what happens to come along, each man for himself. You can't make it be special. What I've always done is to take things with me and make something of them. Everybody does this and in their own way and with no one else. I wish you joy, you're young and if you move carefully and see what you want then there's no limit. Just keep asking anything that comes to your mind and keep pushing. But I just don't have anything to say to anyone who has bright ideas about changing things. I just don't have anything to contribute. It's a crazy old world. I don't consider this as in any way special except as a stop sign. Each one has to try and do what they want to do but they can't count on different people to show them different things. That's too bad, if it lets us down with a thud at the end of this. But each year is a little more truce than the year before, and I lose interest because I'm in another part of the country.

"Companionship is however you make it. You try to make it come back to you the way you like, and if it does, fine, and if it doesn't.

"But this is something that you turn back and toss into the wastebasket.

"And I never was one to go behind the curtains and do everything right.

"But there might be a time when someone will be needing something.

"All my family has gone home now."

A few days later, Amy was released.

I took her for a drive one day in my old Valiant.

"Just seeing things," she said, looking out the window, "makes everything different."

Sitting beside me as we drove, she chatted away out the window and suddenly said in a louder voice: "I've never been so sick as that, never this far, I just didn't know what to plan for and I could always figure things, read them up and down and in and out, and there was someone to say uh-*huh* dearie, there's the hill and there's the bottom and you could see how things would be, and when you go as far south as you can you have to stop and look around before you go on. And sometimes someone can help you see, they can read it better than you because you're lazy and you can't move just then, I'll never forget that."

Gazing out the window, she began to sing in a playful, exaggerated falsetto her own version of a Nina Simone song, laughing at the end of it:

> *I used to be the only one*
> *Now I'm the sad and lonely one*
> *Ain't I blue*
> *Ain't I blue.*

*LAUREL RUST*
*Vol. 9#2&3, 1986*

*Disguises of a Raven's Night*     *lead pencil*     ELOUISE ANN CLARK
*60" x 36"*
*Vol. 7#2, 1982*

*Ancient America I*                    *colored ink*                    *MARY RILEY*
                                        *20" x 13"*
                                    *Vol. 4#1, 1979*
                            *Courtesy of Jacques Baruch Gallery*

*Evening Parrot and New Moon*               *acrylic*               *LINDA LOMAHAFTEWA*
                                          *16" x 11"*
                                      *Vol. 8#2, 1984*

*Migration*                      *chalk pastel on rag paper*                      PAULA LUMBARD
                                 *60" x 48"*
                                 *Vol. 7#3, 1983*
                                 *photo by Rountry/Williams*

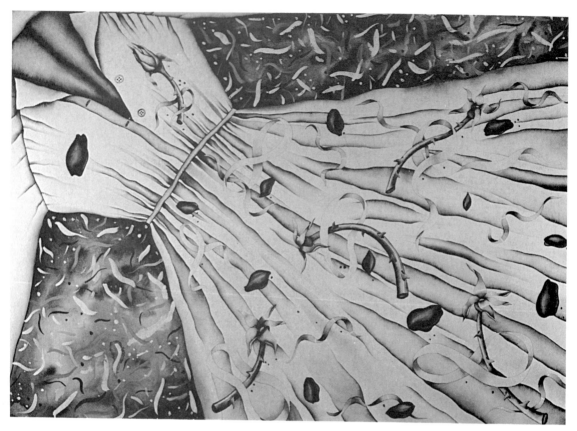

*The Dress*  *watercolor*  *JENNIFER STABLER-HOLLAND*
*40" x 30"*
*Vol. 7#1, 1982*

*The Visitation: Where Should I Put My Suitcase?*     *mixed media*     PATRICIA FORSBERG
$39^3/_8$" x $27^3/_4$"
*Vol. 9#1, 1985*
photo by Jon Schulman
Collection of Bonnie and Denis Phillips

Saint Non's Well           *oil*           *MONICA SJOO*

*Vol. 9#1, 1985*

*On the River Again*  *charcoal*  *CHARLEEN TOUCHETTE*
*35" x 29"*
*Vol. 8#2, 1984*

Lineage       *pencil*       VICKI FOLKERTS-COOTS
*18" x 24"*
*Vol. 2#3, 1978*

*Autorretrato como tehuana*       *oil on masonite*      *FRIDA KAHLO*
24" x 24¾"

*Vol. 5#2&3, 1980*
*photo by Nancy Deffebach*
*Collection of Mr. and Mrs. Jacques Gelman*

*Woman with Fire*                    *etching*                    *ESTER HERNANDEZ*
                                     *14" x 18"*
                                     *Vol. 8#2, 1984*

*Bye Bye Birdie*　　　　*oil on canvas*　　　　MARY HATCH
*28" x 36"*
*Vol. 5#1, 1980*

Latin America: Timeless Time     *acrylic*     BETTY LADUKE
*54" x 68"*
*Vol. 10#1, 1986*

*The Cassowary's Child*     *color etching*     BETTY LADUKE
*15" x 22"*
*Vol. 5#1, 1980*

*P*lants grow, bloom, bear fruit, and shed their
seeds. Birds and animals eat the fruit and spread the seed. Wind catches
seeds blowing them to distant places. Rain falls, moistening the seeds.
They sprout and grow new plants. Plants nurture and protect the planet.

Domesticity and home life have been trivialized as inappropriate subject
matter for literature and art. Women's bodies have been stripped of power and
presented as sexual objects for men's desires and for men's possession.

Sisters, mothers, grandmothers have been important models for women.
In this section the intimate, personal matters that form the basis of human
struggle are addressed: birth and family, sex and death—the reflecting, refract-
ing, magnifying energy of generations of women; the power of a woman's body
and the beauty of female sexual energy; the quest for symbiosis in our relationships with lovers and the world.

# BIRTHING

on the dark side I slip

like silk through night and chaos
wind splinters my hair
peacocks stalking
wild and sensuous as jewels
I see earth through their eyes
past bursting patterns
milestones
flashing at utmost speed

O I hear the light

*MARY TALLMOUNTAIN*
*Vol. 2#3, 1978*

## HAVING GIVEN BIRTH

for the first time

my body comes back
to itself

Spine, half
a wish bone
doubles back
victorious

Stretch marks on my breasts
fade pale
as milk

Around my head songs
from my childhood quiver
like moths, they ask
to be taken back
They ask forgiveness
for having been gone so long

Through my own lips
my mother's voice
sings my daughter to sleep

When she sleeps
at my breast, I become
the oldest person
I have ever known

I am younger than I can remember.

*INGRID WENDT*
*Vol. 2#3, 1978*

(WHEN SHE IS 18, OF WHICHEVER MOON)

(When she is 18, of whichever moon)
she, the daughter, goes out into the car
shuts the car door,
maybe waves to the parents;
she leaves.

Or she, the daughter, flies out the window,
or climbs down the ladder at night,

or she goes so deeply into her room that she's gone. They, the parents, send someone
in to search but never find her. She's left.

In one way or another the daughter leaves, she must, no way out of it.
The daughter leaves at 18: some are 18 earlier; some are 18 later.

Whenever it is that she hits 18 the house shrinks, she bumps her head on the ceiling,
she must slouch to fit in, her elbows knock the windows out. The mother is upset
at this: she, the mother, screams and cries and tells the daughter to get more sleep.
The father is angry and hollers and stomps. The mother, composing herself, tells
the daughter for the one hundredth time to stop slouching. At this time she,
the daughter, looks down to see them: they, the parents, have gotten so short
she can't hear what they're saying. So she pushes the roof off of it, the house,
and squeezes out. That's one way it happens. In any case, the daughter leaves.

(And usually, by the way, it, the house, has by the way dropped into her pocket,
backpack or purse in her process of leaving, and, unwittingly, she carries it
around with her. Until, as often happens, but not always happens, she, the daughter,
perhaps gets a daughter, at which time she, the mother, pulls out the house,
blows it up, all in proportion, rearranges the furniture, and she, the mother,
puts it around her, the baby daughter, and keeps it up for 18 years,)

                                                                        no end.


*JANA ZVIBLEMAN*
*Vol. 9#1, 1985*

## JEWISH MOTHER

*for Della*

I will dance at your wedding
in spite of gout & 200 lbs.
Indian fakirs walk on
nails in their ecstasy.
Daughter this tradition
is in my blood;
it cannot be a stately dance.
my pendulous anatomy will
defy gravity, though you play
rock music I will hear
the Russian Kazatsky
wild & beating in my eardrums
I shall leap like the Slavic
bear in rippling girth,
the world & the moment
may pass in review—
my love will sustain me;
should I die before you marry,
I pledge my honor to dance
at your wedding, I will come
from eons, frost & stars
you will hear violins & tambourines
radiance will be your destiny.

*PEARL BOND*
*Vol. 7#1, 1982*

## MI ESTOMAGO (MY BELLY)

Naked and as if in silence
I approach my belly
it has gone on changing like summer
withdrawing from the sea
or like a dress that expands with the hours
My belly
is more than round
because when I sit down
it spreads like a brush fire
then,
I touch it to recall
all the things inside it:
salt and merriment
the fried eggs of winter breakfasts
the milk that strangled me in my youth
the coca-cola that stained my teeth
the nostalgia for the glass of wine
we discovered in *La Isla*
or french fries and olive oil
And as I remember
I feel it growing
and bowing down more and more ceremoniously to the ground
until it caresses my feet, my toes
that never could belong to a princess,

I rejoice
that my belly is as wide as Chepi's old sombrero—
Chepi was my grandmother—
and I pamper it no end
when it complains or has bad dreams
from eating too much.

Midsummer, at seventy years of age,
this Sunday the seventh
my belly is still with me
and proudly goes parading along the shore
some say I am already old and ugly
that my breasts are entangled with my guts
but my belly is here at my side a good companion
and don't say it's made of fat
rather tender morsels of meat toasting in the sun.

*MARJORIE AGOSIN*
Translated by *COLA FRANZEN*
*Vol. 9#2&3, 1986*

## SISTAH FLO

She carried
one daughter
four sons
nine grandchildren
before a stroke
smoothed her clean
as the white lady's sheets
she scrubbed by hand
for thirty years.
She graced the pews
of Gethsemane every Sunday
sang in tongues to Jesus
about catching arthritis
from between the cracks
stretching less than pennies
sewing thread over thread
laying a brutal husband
to fitful final rest.
She loved through
the eye of a needle
and let Jesus soothe her
as she knew he could
even though she
could not hold a note.

*TERRI L. JEWELL*
*Vol. 9#2&3, 1986*

## WIDOW'S WALK

The Indiana road curves north,
Its steady flatness unrelieved
Until that Eastern shape appears.
A father, suitor struck a bargain:
This house was built to buy a bride
Who yearned for sea spray, beachgrass, sails.
Twelve over twelve in balanced sashes,
Above the doors the windows fan:
The light divides through handmade panes.
Brick chimneys thrusting powerfully
Enclose an inland widow's walk,
Ringed with heavy metal railings,
High in the middle of the roof.

Wrought iron pressed her, thigh and hip,
While far below, lilac blossoms,
Transplanted stock she rooted there,
Pulsed softly in narrow sunlight circles.
High summer's grain grew thick and full
In a sultry, ripening wind.
Corn hardened toward the harvesting.
Crops of winter wheat were sown.

Prairie skies, rolling furrows,
Billowing endlessly in time,
Bound her on that parapet.

She stood alone.

Her hand poised on those sharpened points
That bordered firmly all her life.

She watched that earth.

Her husband, sons tended the farm.
Her daughters married, bore their kind.

She knew the heartland in her bone,
The landscape, in her female flesh:
Semen staining fragile lace,
Birthing blood on bridal linen.
Breaking always on her ear,
Drifting always in her mind,
Sounds of foaming waves and tides,
Cries of white gulls on the shore.

Each day she climbed the worn steps
That took her to her widow's walk,
The only place where she was free
To measure in that smallest space,
Her essence, the stark vacancy.

*DARLENE MATHIS-EDDY*
*Vol. 1#2, 1976*

## SPEAKING IN TONGUES

Mother, I wanted the implant to change
your vision, to let the light shine in.
You and I, Mother, have never seen eye to eye.

I was there when you came out of surgery.
"It was awful," you said. "Just awful.
They didn't put me to sleep."
You were so honest I wanted to cry.

I could have fought for you. But Mother,
just think. Asleep you would never know
if they cut into your heart, the marrow
of your bones. Imagine strangers probing
the pieces for malignancy or other deviations.
They would tell me, Mother. I am your daughter.

In the waiting room I count flowers
painted into a still life, give mother back
her illusions with no black and blue spots.

I could build mother a nest from old creeds,
Martin Luther's hymns. She can weave
fine tatting into the Hippocratic oath.
With one good eye she can work the shuttle,
fix the hard knots. She can be the soloist
in the Hallelujah Chorus when the stone
rolls away and the vision of Jesus appears.

After recovery, I watch my mother
put the doctor back on his pedestal,
caress the dull eye with pancake make-up.
The minister comes to call. Praise the Lord.
My mother is restored, the Republican party
is alive and well, Grandpa, still a saint.
I watch her count the greeting cards,
arrange the new flowers and check
her outlook in the mirror. Amen.

Mother, I wanted you to look at me.
They tell me I speak with my eyes.
For one moment I saw you real
and you were afraid. Look me in the eye,
Mother. Let's not speak in tongues.
You have survived and I am afraid.

*MARILYN FOLKESTAD*
*Vol. 10#1, 1986*

YELLOW JACKETS                                              *JAN CLAUSEN*

*for Phyllis Shannon Clausen, who told me stories*

Month: July. Time: evening. Place: the outskirts of a small midwestern town. Picture a squat, square, ugly red brick house. On its screened-in porch two old women, neighbors, sit: the guest, Mrs. Frederick Baxter (Gertrude), heavily rocking; her hostess, Mrs. Joseph Biehler (Laura), by her own fault suffering in the straight-backed chair. *I've sworn for twenty years I'd buy another; will I die without seeing two comfortable chairs on my porch?*

From a curtained window weak light leaks over the yard; there is a ragged heave of lawn toward the unsidewalked street. Fill in a background of insect noise; low, furtive-seeming murmurs of passersby; infrequent flash of head-lights. Remember the heat, always the heat, so basic that it almost goes un-noticed: a fact, dimension, condition of this existence, indelible as depression or dangerous fever.

*The morning all undone, over and over, every day I woke, the neat package of evening all untied that gave me such satisfaction when I'd washed up from supper and the children were in bed. Oh, morning is a terrible time, the time of unmaking, and yet I believe I still loved morning best, icehats on the milk bottles, the cold cold clink of them; coffee, and Joe just getting started in his truck. I who am finished, undone; I who ought to be ready.*

Like flies around a pot of strawberry jam, she is saying. Or yellow jackets, more like yellow jackets. A bunch of yellow jackets round the table at those family picnics in the county park. Such pesky creatures, moving off a little when you'd shoo them, then coming right back. And all that food, you know how it is with the Germans.

I know just what you mean, Mrs. Baxter sympathizes, about yellow jackets. We had them something awful on the Fourth this year.

Once, Mrs. Biehler continues, when Mavis was three, she tried to catch a yellow jacket and it bit her. I'll never forget her screaming, and the heat, and Joe's mother scowling at me. I must have been expecting Joey, too, at the time; I recall feeling quite nauseous. This was unusual for Mavis, she was generally so quiet, much more so than Joey of course *(poor little Joey)*, or even Lucille *(marrying as she did)*. Till finally I lost my temper and slapped her good.

Mrs. Baxter allows she's glad the Fourth's over with. She is always happy, of course, to see the children; but she gets so tired.

The children, snorts Mrs. Biehler, the children indeed. *A string of female names: Mavis and Lucille; Jo Ellen, Maxine, Rosemary, Mona. At first I thought it* was just coincidence, them all of a sudden buzzing and swarming and pestering me to death. *Mavis in Minneapolis, Lucille in Los Angeles, Jo Ellen in Madison, Rosemary in Des Moines, Maxine you never know from week to week, Mona in my spare bedroom, not moaning yet.* Just another stage, as Mavis always claimed when hers were little.

Well, this is what we have to expect at our age, Laura, Mrs. Baxter mentions. This is what we have to look forward to. From here on I suppose even third and fourth cousins will be showing an interest. At least I can be grateful for my Charlotte.

But that's not it with me, Gert, Mrs. Biehler points out, trying hard to be tactful. Lucille, of course, is quite nicely fixed up. And even Mavis does well with her settlement. No, it isn't money, it's how they look at me, all these expensive long distance phone calls and sudden visits. It's Maxine coming down for the weekend, it's Jo Ellen driving all the way from Madison to play that tape for me when I'd told her plain enough I didn't want to hear it. It's Rosemary going through my cupboards.

Did she do that? Mrs. Baxter eagerly cries. My Charlotte would never.

She certainly did, confirms Mrs. Biehler, grim. And no permission asked. Granny, she says to me, like a little girl all excited, this is Depression Glass! It ought to be, I says, I got it in the Depression.

See what I mean, that stuff is worth money now, Mrs. Baxter nods.

You know how I feel, her friend continues, I feel just like some beat-up old dress that they fish out of the fifty cents bin at the Goodwill and hang up on the antiques rack for fifty dollars. Just because I have lasted. *And I won't even speak of Maxine, with her hair chopped off like you'd cut it with a lawn mower, and calling herself Mavisdaughter when her name is Larson, never mind what unpleasantness her father has caused.*

Can't they see, Mrs. Baxter laments, that a person's got little enough to keep them while they're alive and bury them decently, after? Don't they have eyes? But no. They figure better safe than sorry, I suppose. Calling up to ask would I like to be read to! Oh, I am grateful for Charlotte.

Even Lucille has started in, admits Mrs. Biehler, Lucille, who never was a whiner. Writing me letters on her artistic note paper: Wouldn't you like to come out for a little vacation, maybe spend the winter? Arthur and I will be happy to send the tickets. Though perhaps she feels guilty, dumping Mona on me. *A funny, sullen little thing, Mona.*

Well, why not go, says pragmatic Mrs. Baxter. After all, Los Angeles.

I've been already, Mrs. Biehler reminds her. Oh, it is true I haven't seen my grandson in seven years. *In his pictures he slightly appears to resemble my Joey.*

David? Mrs. Baxter's interest quickens. What's David doing these days?

I cannot say I am fond of California, Mrs. Biehler firmly continues, prefer-ring to disregard the question. *You wouldn't want to know, Gran, was what Mona answered me when I asked her how he is filling up this year he took off from college. Joey dead already, at his age.* Besides, Gert, don't you see what I'm getting at?

No, Laura, what? begs plodding Mrs. Baxter.

That it is only another form of pestering on the part of Lucille and them, her friend concludes, triumphant. Would you care for some cake? I'm afraid it's only Sara Lee from the supermarket.

In this heat, Laura? I've lost my appetite. But I'll have a spot of iced tea, if you can spare it.

Of course, says Mrs. Biehler, reach me your glass.

Oh don't get up, she cries reflexively; but her comparatively spry hostess is already well on her way to the kitchen.

I take Sweet 'n Low, she therefore hollers out.

Goodness, Gert, after all these years don't you think I'd remember? Mrs. Biehler's voice continues through the open window, over a clink of glasses.

And even Mavis she says *(good little Mavis)*, who's supposed to be taking courses to keep her busy, comes around here all at loose ends asking is there anything she can do. Reminds me of rainy days when the children were little. How I dreaded rain! You ought to be growing up on the farm like me, I'd tell them, you'd never ask what to do. Then I'd make Mavis dust, or iron handker-chiefs. *Moving through those high, light rooms on Chestnut Street. How I loved those rooms.* Lucille, most often, could think up some game to play, and of course there wasn't much work for a boy around the house, so Joey got off easy. Here's your iced tea, Gert. Have you been following this in the papers about how Sweet 'n Low is supposed to cause cancer?

At our age, Laura, what difference can it make? Mrs. Baxter calmly reasons, getting a firm grip on the sweating glass. Besides, I tend towards diabetes. Perhaps you're right; it's something other than money yours are after.

No, it's not money they're after, with all their pestering. *Oh, she has a poor opinion of my daughters, Lucille marrying a Jew, and Mavis, of course, being divorced now.* Do you find you feel the heat worse as you get older? I believe I do. *And of all five grandchildren, not a one like her Charlotte, married to an electrician, maybe, but so helpful, so sweet.*

I'm sure I do, affirms Mrs. Baxter. And don't it look like this spell would last forever? Maybe we'll get some rain tonight, though. So Mona is staying the summer, is she now?

Yes, her friend replies, concealing considerable uneasiness. *Mona is going through a difficult time, Lucille wrote.* Yes, she has decided.

Mrs. Baxter observes that it must be a trial, having someone always under foot like that.

Well, I can't say she's any help to me, but she keeps herself to herself. She's no hindrance, either, like some people I could mention. *She is extremely secretive and does not want to discuss her problems with me, Lucille went on. Of course the end of high school is often a difficult time for today's youngsters, so I don't worry.* Although she smokes, such a terrible filthy habit. *Perhaps spending a few weeks with you will give her the opportunity she needs to get herself on a better footing.* But it's good to know there's someone in the house, if anything should happen.

I know what you mean, Mrs. Baxter agrees quickly. Why, ever since poor Winifred's accident seems like I've been afraid to so much as go down cellar for a jar of jam. Is it because of Arthur that you prefer not to go to Los Angeles?

Mrs. Biehler assures her that's water under the bridge. *Though I will admit neither Joe nor I were happy when Lucille came home one day and announced she would be marrying this Arthur Moskowitz, a would-be college professor from Chicago.* Arthur is a good man, she emphasizes. The Jews are fine people. *And how we argued, Lucille reminding me that Father tried to stop me marrying Joe. But this is different, I tried to make her see.*

You may be right, I'm sure, concedes Mrs. Baxter, but something like this you never really quite get over, all the same. Take when my Eula married that twice-divorced fellow, and her not out of high school.

Yet look what came of it, Mrs. Biehler cries. *With us, I told her, it was following the War, and of course there was still considerable feeling against the Germans. But at least Joe was a Christian, and not a Roman Catholic either. I would not have married a Catholic.* Didn't Eula have Charlotte by that man? Could you ask for better than Charlotte? *Though I can never rightfully blame Lucille, after what I almost did. It was just she came so close on Joey, and I was tired.*

Of course Charlotte is a comfort, assents Mrs. Baxter. Still—poor Eula. How hard it is to watch your children suffer.

Oh isn't it, isn't it, Mrs. Biehler mourns. *I went so far as to get the name of a St. Paul doctor that did such things. Worried half to death thinking how I could keep it from Joe. In the end, of course, I couldn't get the money.* To think of my mother, who buried three of us, not counting the one or two that was born dead. *Where Lucille is concerned, I feel I have only myself to blame.* I don't suppose I'll ever get over Joey. I know Joe never did. *Though our church no longer holds that it is a sin.*

You never really do, Mrs. Baxter agrees.

When Joe passed away, last thing he called for Joey. *There are times now I feel I should have had more than the three.* And he looked up, and there was Lucille standing. You know how tall she is. And confused, like he was, he decided she was Joey. So he was satisfied, anyway.

I am glad to know Joe went easy, Mrs. Baxter says. I surely wish the same for my poor Fred.

Have you been to see him? her friend makes ritual inquiry. *But who could have guessed there'd be another War? So young Joey looks in his uniform in that picture.*

Yes, sighs Mrs. Baxter, yesterday. He was asleep, though; they tell me he sleeps the better part of the time. Even when he's awake he don't know me, of course. Poor Fred.

At least he is not in pain, observes Mrs. Biehler, rather troubled. *I so much did not want to be like Mother.*

Mrs. Baxter agrees that this is a blessing; ventures, after a moment, that it seems to be cooling off a little and perhaps she would have a piece of the cake that was mentioned.

By all means, says Mrs. Biehler; I'm happy to get it out of the house. I tend to nibble, and I shouldn't have it, not with my weight. I keep telling Mona not to buy it. Of course she's thin as a rail.

Your weight, scoffs Mrs. Baxter. Laura, look at me!

Oh, go on, Gertrude! (but Mrs. Biehler is pleased). I'm fatter than I look, it's just I know how to dress. And how is your blood pressure these days? What does the doctor say?

About the same, Mrs. Baxter admits, taking a forkful of cake. Of course I'm on the medication still. This cake really is not bad at all for store bought. But maybe you should get Mona to make you a nice coffee cake from scratch. Charlotte does that for me sometimes, it's not so much trouble.

I'm afraid Mona is perfectly useless in a kitchen. *You'll see soon enough, it's different, I said to her. It's different with a little one, there's no getting around it.* To tell you the truth, I'd rather not turn her loose in there. Who knows what sort of mess she'd make?

At least, Mrs. Baxter hints broadly, she might learn a thing or two she will need to know one day.

Perhaps; but I'm not running a cooking school. Let Lucille teach her, with her Chinese cooking lessons, since pot roasts and simple baking like I showed my girls seem to be insufficient, Mrs. Biehler replies rather bitterly.

Chinese? Mrs. Baxter raises heavy eyebrows.

Chinese, repeats Mrs. Biehler. Fifteen dollars a lesson, I think she wrote it cost her.

Well, says Mrs. Baxter, shaking her head in sympathetic sorrow, she's got that kind of money, I suppose.

Mrs. Biehler is reminded somehow of her other problems. Did I tell you Maxine showed up over the weekend, not bothering to telephone? she inquires. And Jo Ellen was here with her tape machine, after I made it clear I wasn't interested? Maxine did not look at all pleased when she saw Jo Ellen.

What's this, cries Mrs. Baxter, they don't get along?

Apparently not, admits Mrs. Biehler. I asked Mavis about it; I'll explain later. Anyway, they have this thing called the Women's Something-or-Other Project, something to do with history, over there at the University where Jo Ellen is trying to get tenure.

Trying to get *what?*

That's all right, Gertrude, Mrs. Biehler reassures her, I wouldn't know of it myself if Arthur hadn't been through it. *Two professors in the family now.* It means the teacher has a permanent job, can't be fired.

Why, what an outlandish idea! marvels Mrs. Baxter. What if they stopped showing up to work?

Mrs. Biehler allows she never thought of that. It does sound kind of funny, she concedes, but Jo Ellen explained it to me, how it's important for freedom of speech and such. Anyway, she wants it awful bad. And she says it's harder for a woman to get it.

Like everything else, Mrs. Baxter generalizes. But then, of course the men would need the jobs most. Do you suppose Jo Ellen will ever get married?

Who knows? Here I will be seventy-eight in October. *And Mona's condition I cannot even mention.* Mrs. Biehler looks so upset that Mrs. Baxter, alarmed, tactfully returns the conversation to the subject of Jo Ellen's tape recorder.

Well, she explains, apparently this project involves Jo Ellen going around tape recording women our age talking over their memories. From what she told me, it isn't helping her get that tenure she wants, since the higher-ups say she should be writing articles about books by men.

Some people don't know which side their bread's buttered on, Mrs. Baxter observes pointedly.

My thought exactly, her friend agrees. Jo Ellen, I told her, I think you are being foolish. I think you had better make up your mind, do you want this tenure, or not? But she didn't answer me; she just laughed and turned on that machine, though I had informed her several times I wasn't interested.

And what was on it? Mrs. Baxter is perhaps too eager.

A woman talking, replies Mrs. Biehler with distaste. Though she had such a thick accent—Polish, I would judge—that it was hard to understand her. First she told about places she had worked in, filthy sweat shops and such. Then she got real personal, and went on about having relations with her husband and all, and the times her babies were born. *It made me nearly sick to hear it, thinking of Mother.* Perhaps the Poles don't mind discussing such things, but I could never. *I promised myself I'd never be like her, with a belly like an old sack of potatoes, and always so tired.*

You mean you want me to say a bunch of stuff like that, and then you are going to play it for total strangers? I asked Jo Ellen. *One time I remember watching for the Doctor, I couldn't have been more than six or seven, hearing her, praying so hard for him to hurry. Praying to see him riding up that road.* But she claims many women are glad to talk to her. They start remembering things they'd all but forgotten, she tells me. *Hearing her moan and scream in that back room; too many of us, by then, to be sent to the neighbors.* They're so glad to have somebody to talk with, according to Jo Ellen.

Well, I says, I'm not so hard up, thank goodness. Even if I did have such frightful things to tell. And as for what people have forgotten, sometimes they have their reasons. But we need your stories, Granny, Jo Ellen starts in, like a youngster begging for candy.

If that ain't the limit! Mrs. Baxter exclaims.

I could have slapped her, Mrs. Biehler agrees. I could see she was getting impatient with me, too, though she was trying not to show it. Do you keep a diary, Granny? she says to me. Of course not, I says, what earthly good would that be? *Not mentioning my flower garden journal, which I've never showed anyone.* Your life isn't just your private property, you know, she says. *Looking at me with that same covetous look Rosemary had when she spied the set of Bauer dishes I have in the cupboard, the ones I use for everyday, and she said to me, Granny, do you know, they sell a plate like this for ten dollars in the shops in Des Moines?*

Whose property is it, then, I'd like to know? I inquired of Jo Ellen. And what would you young women want with it anyway? You're liberated, you don't need my stories. Don't you have jobs and TV dinners and frozen waffles and Pampers and ways to get out of having babies, for that matter? Don't you have tenure? I said to her.

Not yet I don't, she answered me back. And then Maxine had to get into it. It's Granny's story, she informs Jo Ellen. She shouldn't have to talk if she doesn't want to.

Of course not, Jo Ellen says, with that phony smile. Well, Granny, I think

I will take my tape machine and go. I have quite a drive back to Madison, after all.

Maxine was prepared to stay the night. But I was so worn out with their bickering, I wanted to be quiet. So I reminded her Mona was using the spare room. *I will write them a letter, Gran, she said to me, but I would like to remain here till the end of August.* I had a headache from listening to all that, and my arthritis was bothering me something dreadful. *Mona, I said, you've got to listen to reason.* Mona, of course, is so quiet it's almost like being alone. *Are you telling me I should get rid of it, Gran, because I'm not going to, Mona said. Not this time. Don't worry, I'll go home before I start to show, your neighbors won't know a thing.* But later, when Mavis called, I asked her about the girls.

And what is the problem between them? Mrs. Baxter interjects, feeling rather out of her league but desirous of conveying sympathy.

According to Mavis, Mrs. Biehler explains, Jo Ellen calls herself a radical feminist, whatever that may be. *They are used to little bastards in L.A., said Mona.* But she is still willing to associate with men under some circumstances. *Young lady, I mentioned, kindly watch your language.*

I should hope so, Mrs. Baxter observes, or how can she expect to meet a future husband? What about Maxine?

Well, elaborates Mrs. Biehler, Maxine, according to Mavis, is more radical even than that. *In '34 when they had that terrible strike, Joe was all set to go up to Minneapolis.* Though it was plain enough to me she didn't much care to discuss it. *Full of swagger, and talk about the Working Man.* While Rosemary, Mavis claims, is not the least bit radical. *Oh, how I had to beg him not to go, as later I begged Joey.*

In my day, I hinted, a radical meant a Red. *Joe, please Joe, we have a chance, I said, we have a chance.* I hope, I said to Mavis, that neither Jo Ellen nor Maxine are doing anything foolish. *And I was right, in the long run, wasn't I?*

Oh goodness, no, Mother, don't worry about that, says Mavis. *We got this place all paid for, didn't we? And Doctors and Professors in the family, for what they're worth. Though Joe had to slave for others all his life.*

I let Mavis know I'm aware Rosemary has been living with her young man. I didn't know you knew, she says, embarrassed.

Of course I knew, I says. Just because I may wear bifocals doesn't mean I'm completely blind, not yet. I know how the young people tend to think these days, and I made a couple inquiries of Jo Ellen.

I hope they get married soon. I think it is likely, said Mavis (*always the good one*) in that little voice of hers, like I might hit her, though I never struck the children. *Not like Mother, making us cut the switches.*

I don't really see why she should, Mavis, I pointed out, considering the example she has to look to. *Who could have imagined, when Mavis married a Doctor, he'd end unzipping his pants in front of little girls in schoolyards?*

Mother, please, says Mavis, so sensitive. *And Joe so proud of her, on their wedding day.*

And where does Maxine come by her means of support? I took the opportunity to inquire, being that we were on the subject of the children. Mavis, I figured, was probably giving her money. *Mavis, good; but softer than biscuit dough.*

Oh, Mavis said, she is presently looking for work. She and her friend Cindy share their income.

That's odd, isn't it, I said. Two girls.

Here Mrs. Baxter, used to these harangues, ventures she wouldn't mind another smidgen of that cake. I can see what you're saying about that tape machine, she quickly adds. It would be an embarrassment.

Oh, indecent, indecent. I never could have done it, says Mrs. Biehler.

But then, Mrs. Baxter muses, you wouldn't be obliged to tell about anything you didn't want to.

Gertrude Baxter! Mrs. Biehler protests.

Well, she confesses, it would give a person someone to talk to. I'm not like you, Laura, I don't enjoy being alone.

But what about Charlotte? urges Mrs. Biehler.

Charlotte is sometimes busy with those two babies. Besides, there are a few things I'd like to preserve for future generations.

Such as, Gertrude? the other prompts, severely.

Recipes, Mrs. Baxter defensively murmurs, recipes and things.

Recipes! Recipes is hardly the kind of thing Jo Ellen would want to hear about, Mrs. Biehler is driven to explain. *I did not tell her I write about my flowers.* If you've got recipes, hand them down to Charlotte.

But these aren't ordinary recipes, they're fancy, things my mother taught me special, pleads Mrs. Baxter. She didn't teach none of my sisters, only me. And Charlotte, while being a good cook, is only a plain cook. Besides, I doubt that she would have the time. That husband of hers, you know, can be quite demanding.

But don't you see, Mrs. Biehler cries, thoroughly exasperated, that cooking is just the sort of thing young women like Jo Ellen have absolutely no time for or interest in? *You'll see soon enough, I told Mona, how things will change. Babies require a clean place to play, after all, and clean clothing, and food to eat, which can't come out of a jar forever.* Aren't you aware that this is what they think is wrong with us, that we spent too much time cooking and cleaning and having babies? *You shouldn't have them if you plan not to lift a finger, I said to her, after all you needn't, abortion is perfectly legal, I read the papers.* Of course they haven't the faintest notion what it was like for us, no washing machines or daycare. No mixes or Sara Lee packaged cake back then, for sure.

*Calm down, Gran, it's bad for your heart, Mona said. And there's something in her voice that calms me, I don't know what.*

*But have you ever stopped to consider? I said. Do you find the answers in your Buddhist books?*

*Hey Gran, she said, with her funny little smile. And I do believe I prefer the way she calls me Gran to the others, with their Granny, Granny, Granny, like I was one of those silly dustmop dresses, or a pair of spectacles. She stubbed out her cigarette and she took my hand, all aching and twisted up with the arthritis, and laid it on her stomach, that's still as flat as flat, though not for long.*

*Never mind about the cooking and the cleaning, she said. Let's don't borrow trouble, okay, Gran?*

*What a funny, old-fashioned thing for her to say.*

Well, of course I would have no way to know all this, being that there are no university professors in my family, replies Mrs. Baxter with considerable dignity. Since the young women of my acquaintanceship seem content to have babies like everybody else. But would you simply mention my name to Jo Ellen?

Mrs. Biehler regards her disapprovingly. *I'm seventy-seven and still not ready to die.*

You might tell her I will give her some additional information, if only she will record my recipes, Mrs. Baxter insists.

I will mention it, Mrs. Biehler concedes at last (*I have had it so much easier than my mother, how is it I am still not satisfied?*), helping herself to a generous slice of cake.

*JAN CLAUSEN*
Vol. 4#1, 1979

Even though she always has peppermint in her apron pockets, nobody much visits Grandma any more. Once in a while my brother, Buster, stops by to pick me up and we go out to the flats to see her. Or someone who has moved away returns to town on their summer vacation to look over their old homeplace, trying to pick up the lost pieces of their lives, wanting stories about their kin. They stop by to ask my grandmother where old so-and-so has gone. More often than not, she directs them to the cemetery, peppermint candy in their hands.

"That bag goes out to the car." I point at the brown paper sack. Buster moves the coleus plants and the clay sheep that has grass sprouting from its back like green wool. He snoops in the bag. "The cookies are in the cupboard," I tell him.

He opens the cupboard and rummages around for the Oreos. I have just enamelled the kitchen and the cabinet doors stick. "Leave them open," I say to Buster. I inspect the kitchen before leaving for Grandma's. It passes my scrutiny, the clean blue paint and the new tablecloth I made of white strawberry-printed cotton.

We pack up Buster's Chevy with my clothes, the groceries, my dog Teddy, and the radio I bought for Grandma. We drive past the Dunkard Brethren Church. There are some people, perhaps the choir, standing outside in dark robes. I think we look pretty flashy, passing by in the gold Chevrolet with shining chrome, and bumperstickers saying *Indian Affairs are the Best*, and *Pilgrim, Go Home.* I sit very straight with my eyelids lowered even though inside my body I am exhilarated, enjoying this ride in my brother's car. We drive past the stand of scrub oak and then turn off the paved road into the silence that exists between towns. The crows fly up off the road, cursing at us. Since his wife isn't along, Buster accelerates and lets the car go almost as fast as it will, "tying on the tachs." We speed along. "I clocked her at one ten," he says. He slows down by the cornfields and paces himself on out through the flatlands where Grandma lives. It has been raining and everything is moist and bright, the outlines of the buildings cleaner than usual. When we pull off the road at Grandma's I stay in the car a few minutes to look at the morning glories she has planted. They are blooming, the blue flowers on a vined arch over the old front door. The Heaven Blue circles nod in the ozone-smelling breeze.

Teddy is anxious to get out and go searching for moles. He whines and paces across the back seat. "Let that damn dog out," Buster says, but he opens the door before I can turn around and get to it. Teddy runs out barking, his tail pulling him sideways with joy. Grandma hears. She comes to the door and stands waiting in the shade, surrounded by the morning glories on her front steps. She already has her hand in her apron pocket, ready to lure us with peppermint, when Teddy turns and circles back viciously, barking at a car that has pulled up silently behind us. I didn't hear the limousine drive up and now Teddy is all around it, barking and raging at the waxed, shining dark metal of the car, and at its tires that remain, miraculously, clean, even driving through the mud.

"Theodore!" I yell out his proper name, reserved for reprimands and orders. Teddy continues to bark, his golden tail down between his short Dingo legs, his claws digging into wet red clay. The chauffeur ignores him and goes around stiffly to open the back car door.

Grandma is taking it all in, looking proud and pompous. She respects money but she hates those people who have it. All money is dirty, she has said. It all started with the Rockefellers and their ilk. Now she remains standing very straight and tall, her hand still in the blue-flowered pocket, while a woman is let out of the car and begins walking across the chicken yard. The white woman's shoes are expensive. They are rich beige leather and I feel tense watching her heels dig into the clay soil and the chicken droppings. The muddy clay tries to suck the woman down. The chickens make a path for her, scurrying off and clucking. A copper hen that has been roosting in a tree falls out and screeches, scurries off muddy, and waddling.

I recognize the lady. She stopped in once for a meal at the Hamburger Heaven where Buster used to work. She was out of place and the customers and employees all stared at her. She made them uneasy and they alternately talked too much and too loud, or they were silent. When the order was ready, Buster took several plates around the room and stopped at the woman's table, flustered. He was overly serious in his discomfort, his face tense. Like an accusation, he said, "You're the Hamburger." I tried to hide my laughter, but it floated up into the entire room.

I step close to hear the conversation between Grandma and the woman. Grandma's jaw is tight like trouble is in the air. While they talk, I pull a stamen from a morning glory and suck it.

"I'd like to buy two dozen eggs," says the beige shoe lady, opening her pocketbook and releasing the odor of French perfume and money.

"We're all out of eggs." Grandma still has her hand in her pocket. She avoids looking at the woman's face. She looks past her at the horizon. It is the way she looks through city people, or people with money, as though they aren't there.

"I'll take a bag of feed then." The woman is thin and wispy. Her hair falls forward as she opens her wallet. The bills are neatly ordered. I can't help but notice Grandma's eyes on them.

"Haven't had any feed delivered from the co-op as late," says Grandma, nonchalantly. Grandma is the local distributor of feed grain and Watkins products, including the cherry-flavored drink mix. She keeps an entire room neatly stocked with bags of grains and bottles of vanilla, aspirin, vitamins, and liniment. And she sells eggs. It is how she supports all those chickens, she claims.

Grandma offers the woman a mint, but the woman refuses it and grows huffy. "Probably the diet type," I hear Buster say under his breath and I'm sure the woman overheard him because she is clearly put out, and says to Grandma, "Why don't you close all the way down or put a sign out?"

"I'm fixing to, once you leave." I can feel a smile under Grandma's words even though her face has no expression and her eyes are blank, staring off into Kansas or some other distant state. The woman does not know she is being made fun of, and she wants something else, I can tell. She wants to help Grandma out, to be good to the poor, or something. It is often that way with the rich. But it seems to me that there are some barriers in life that can't be passed through by good deeds or money. Like the time I found a five dollar bill on the floor of the movie theater and felt guilty for picking it up, felt like a thief. It was a fire in my pocket. On the way home I saw a man going through the trash, collecting cans to cash in. I took out the bill and handed it to him. I said I just found it and maybe it was his. He took it, but there was a dreadful and shameful look on his face and I knew then that everyone ought to stay in their own place, wherever that may be, without trespassing on other people's lives. Maybe money just goes where it wants and leaves the rest of us alone.

But Grandma will not be shamed, even though the house looks dilapidated in contrast to the woman and her car. Grandma is proud enough still to plant the flowers and water them with the blue plastic pitcher.

The woman returns to the limousine and they drive away. If it weren't for the recent rain, the car would have covered the morning glories in a great cloud of dust. I wonder what it is that made the chauffeur so anxious to leave.

"Last week she wanted to buy the house," Grandma says, and takes out two lint-covered peppermint kisses and gives one each to me and Buster.

"This old place?" Buster has no tact. I give him one of my looks which he has said could kill, but he goes on talking. "How much did she offer you? You should have taken it." His cheek is swollen with the peppermint. "You are probably sitting on an oil well."

But Grandma loves her home and will never leave it as long as she lives. Now and then she is in a bad mood and this is going to be one of those times. Her eyes are sullen. I remind myself of her better moments. Out loud I say to Buster, "Remember the day we took Grandma to town? When she was in such a good humor that she went up to that tall policeman and asked, 'Do you know where any trouble is?'"

Buster's smile begins on the left side of his face, but Grandma ignores what I say. She hands me the egg basket. "Sis, why don't you go out and gather up the eggs?"

Teddy is overjoyed to go with me, looking in the corners of the barn, the storage shed, under old tires on the ground. I find a few eggs in new places, in a batch of damp grass, under the morning glories. Teddy runs in circles and the crows fly up around us. They remind me of stories, like how Old Crow Raven used to be white, white snowy feathers, marble white beak and claws, until one day he got too sure of himself and offered to go to an island of fire and bring back a coal for the two-legged, unwinged people. As he descended to the island, following the orange flames and black smoke billowing up from a hollow tree, he was overcome with the heat and blinded by a thick dark cloud of smoke. Disoriented, he flew straight into the flames and was scorched. That is the reason, people say, why the crows are black. Grandma's theory is that the bird went for the wrong reasons. He didn't really care about the people at all. He just wanted to prove his worth.

When I go inside and set the eggs on the table, Grandma is on one of her lectures about how people are just like blackbirds except they are paling. "Money is turning everybody to white," she says. "All the Indians are going white. Oh, I suppose they still care about their little ones and go to church on Sunday, but all they've got their minds on is the almighty dollar." She stops abruptly while I recount the eggs. There are thirty-one of them, and what with yesterday's eggs around the house, she could have sold the woman four dozen or so. She fixes her gaze on me and the whites around her dark pupils startle me. Even the eggs seem to wobble on the unlevel table. "How come you never come to visit anymore? I have a hundred grandchildren and no one ever comes out here." It's no use arguing, so I don't answer.

"They're all trying to make a buck, Grandma," Buster says.

Most of the time Grandma doesn't have anyone to talk to and she gets lonely. All of my cousins have been breaking away like spiders, going to cities, to California, marrying and moving. That's why I brought her the radio.

"I don't want to hear anything about money or bucks." Her jaw is tight. She looks straight at Buster.

I turn on the water in the sink and the sound of it running drowns out Grandma's voice. She is still talking about all the Indians out here acting like white people, and about how no one comes to see her. "Those men bullying their sons," she says. "They shoot the birds right out of the air. And money, I wouldn't touch that stuff if you paid me to." And then she notices the radio and becomes quiet. "What's this?"

I dry my hands and plug it in. "I brought it for you. I thought you might like some music." I turn the station selector. Buster says, "You can talk to *that* thing all you want."

I put it on a gospel station, because that is her favorite music. But it's only a man talking and he has a bad voice. *I know my mother went to heaven, harumph, and I had a brother who died and I know he went to heaven.* The man clears his throat. *One by one, we, uh, proceed, our candles lighted. We, you, you, I, I think that maybe some of those Europeans haven't reached the height of Christianity, harumph, that we have, but maybe we have really gone below them and maybe we have, uh, wronged them.*

Buster imitates a rooster, his fists in his armpits. "Bock, Bock, Begaw," he says. I give him a dirty look.

"Don't you make fun," Grandma says. "The first time I ever heard a radio, don't you know, was Coolidge's inaugural address."

And she starts in again, right over the voice of the radio, about how no one comes to talk to her and how we don't even call her on the telephone. Buster gets angry. He says she's getting senile and he walks out the door and slams it. Grandma and I are silent because he walked out stiff and angry, and the radio says, *I got saved from the sermons you preach, uh, that's what he said, and from the sermons on your pages in the mail.*

I'm still thinking about going to heaven with a candle, but I hear Buster outside, scurrying around. I look out the window but can't tell what he's doing.

When he returns, he is carrying a crow and tracking in red mud. "How did you catch that?" I ask. Its eyes are wild but it is beautiful with black feathers shining like silk and velvet. I go closer to look at it. "Can I touch it?" I put my hand over the bird. "Is it hurt?"

Buster pulls back and looks me in the eye. His look scares me. He is too intense and his eyes are darker than usual. He takes hold of the wing. "Don't," I say, but he grabs that glorious coal-colored wing and twists it.

"Buster!" I yell at him and the crow cries out too.

He throws it down on the floor. I'm too afraid to move. "Now, don't say no one comes to see you. This damn crow won't leave. You can tell him all you want how nobody comes to see you." Buster stalks out and we hear the car engine start. I am standing, still unable to move, looking at the bird turning circles on the floor, and beginning to cry. "Oh, Grandma, how could Buster be so awful?" I go down to pick up the injured bird, but it tries to get away. I don't blame it. There's no reason to be trusting. Grandma is sad too, but she just sits at the table and I know we are both thinking of Buster's cruelty and we are women together for the first time.

I turn off the radio and I am thinking of all the poor earthly creatures.

There is a cardboard box in the Watkins room so I go in to get it for the bird and notice that the room is full of the feed Grandma refused to sell the beige shoe lady.

Grandma has already broken a stick and is fitting it to the bird's wing. It is quiet in her hands. I strip off a piece of red calico cotton from her quilting cloth. She takes it in her wrinkled hand and wraps the smooth wing.

"I hate him," I say. "He's always been mean." But Grandma doesn't say anything. She is busy with the crow and has placed it in the box on a nest of paper towels.

"I guess that's what happens to people who think about money all the time," she says. "They forget about the rest of life. They don't pay mind to the hurts of each other or the animals. But the Bible teaches me not to judge them." Still, she says nothing else about money or visitors.

The crow listens when Grandma talks. For several days it has been nodding its head at her and following her with its eyes. It listens to the gospel radio, too. "That crow is a heartbreaker," she says. "Just look at him." I hope it isn't true. It is a lovely bird and sometimes cries out weakly. He has warm black wings and eyes made of stolen corn. I am not a crow reverencer, but I swear that one night I heard it talking to Grandma and it was saying that no one comes to visit.

Grandma is telling it a story about the crows. "They were people and used to speak our tongues," she tells him and he listens. It is raining outside and the rain is hitting windows. The earth outside is full of red puddles and they are moving. Somewhere outside, a door is slamming open and closed in the wind.

"You'd like that rain water," she tells the crow. "Make your feathers soft."

Though I am mad at Buster, I can see that he was right. This bird and Grandma are becoming friends. She feeds it grain and corn. It rides on her shoulder and is the color her hair used to be. Crow pulls at the strands of her gray hair. It is like Grandma has shed a skin. She is new and soft, a candlelight inside her.

"Bird bones heal pretty fast," she tells me. "Not like ours."

"Can we listen to something besides gospel for a while?" I ask her. She ignores the question so I go into the bedroom to read a magazine and take a nap. The phone rings and I hear Grandmother talking and then the radio goes off and the front door opens and closes. I get up and go out into the kitchen, but it is silent except for the bird picking at the cardboard box.

For a moment I consider putting him out in the rain, splint and all, he looks so forlorn. But Grandma would never forgive me. I ask him, "Have you heard that money is evil?"

Teddy is barking at the front door. It's Buster. Even the dog is unkind to him, growling back in his throat. Buster wants to see if we need anything or if I am ready to go home. I don't speak to him and he sits down on the sofa to read the paper. I stay in the kitchen with Crow.

A house without its tenant is a strange place. I notice for the first time that without Grandma's presence, the house smells of Vicks and old wool. Her things look strange and messy, even the doilies on the couch and end tables are soiled. The walls are sweating and the plaster is stained. I can see Buster sitting on the sofa reading the paper and I decide to tell him I think he is beyond forgiveness.

"Leave me alone." He stands up. His pants ride low and he puts his hands in his pockets and pushes the pants down lower. It is a gesture of intimidation. "She's got company, hasn't she? And maybe that crow will teach her how to behave." He says he is bringing a cage and I say a cage is no place for a wild bird that longs to be outside in the free air. We are about to get into it when Grandma returns. She is crying. "I ought to kill myself," she says.

We grow quiet and both look down at the floor. I have never seen her cry except at funerals, and I sneak glances up at her now and then while she is crying, until she tells me, "Quit gawking. I just lost all my money."

"Your money?" I am struck stupid. I am surprised. I know she never believed in banks and I thought she didn't believe much in money either. I didn't know she had any. I worry about how much she lost. By her tears, I can tell it wasn't just the egg money.

"I hid it in the umbrella because I was scared of robbers, and I lost it in the rain. When I went back looking for it, it wasn't there." She checks inside the wet umbrella, opening and closing it as if she couldn't believe its absence, running her hand around the spokes. "I forgot I hid it there. I just plain forgot," she wails. "I used to keep it in the cupboard until I heard about the burglars."

There is a circle of water around her on the floor and her face is broken, but she takes two pieces of peppermint from her pocket and absently hands one to each of us, the old habit overpowering grief. "I think I should have sold that woman the eggs."

She has a lot of sorrow bending her back. "I walked up the road as fast as I could, but it was already gone."

She becomes as quiet as the air between towns. I turn on the radio and it sounds like a funeral with *We Shall Gather at the River.* Grandma picks up Crow and he seems to leap right to her chest and balance there on one of the old ivory buttons. She reaches into her left pocket and takes out grains of corn.

Grandma's shoes are ruined. She puts them on the stove to dry but they are already curling upward at the toes and the leather soles are coming apart.

"How's your kids, Buster?"

"Pretty good," but he looks glum. He's probably worried about his lost inheritance.

"How's Flora?"

Buster has his ready-made answers. "Well," he drawls, "by the time I met her I knew what happiness was." I chime in, mocking, "But it was too late to do anything about it." I finish the sentence with him. Grandma looks at me, startled, and is silent a moment, and then she begins to laugh.

There's nothing else to do, so I get up. "Grandma, you want some eggs?" I turn on the stove. "I'll cook up some eggs and cornmeal pancakes." I wonder how much money she had hidden away.

"I'm all out of molasses," she says. "Plum out."

"Buster will go to the store and get some. Won't you, Buster?"

"In this rain?" But he looks at me and I look stern. "Oh sure, yeah, I'll be right back." And he carefully folds the paper and picks up his keys and goes to the door. He is swallowed up by the blowing torrents of water.

I take Grandma's shoes off the stove and put them by the back door.

"Edna fell down the stairs last night," Grandma says, an explanation of where she has been. "Broke her hip."

"How is she?"

"I didn't get to see her. Because of the money. Maybe Buster will take me."

I put some batter in the pan and it sizzles. Crow chatters back at it and it sounds like he is saying how hard it is to be old. I want to put my hand on Grandma's shoulder, but I don't. Instead I go to the window and look out. Crow's lovers or cousins are bathing in the puddles of rain water, washing under their wings and shaking their feathers. I think Crow is the one who went to that island after fire, and now, even though his body is so much like the night sky, he is doomed to live another life. I figure he's going to stay here with Grandma to make up for his past mistakes. I think Grandma is right about almost everything. I feel lonely. I go over and touch her. She clasps my hand tightly and then lets go and pats it. "Your pancakes are burning," she says.

*LINDA HOGAN*
*Vol. 8#2, 1984*

She lived in the dining room of a four-bedroom house, now divided into sleeping rooms for graduate students. The kitchen and bathroom were communal. She used deceit when she rented the room from the landlord. Her great-grandson was moving over from Ephrata. He was going to graduate school in hard-rock geology.

But she moved in. Once ensconced, she was ignored by the absent landlord. The students didn't mind her there. They only slept there, studied in their labs and libraries, and spoke to her at least once a month. She didn't like to chat.

She had dined in this room before. Before was when the focal point of the room was a stuffed turkey or a sheet cake with candles and animated space men stalking among sugar roses. Now only a small table held a coffee mug and a bakery sack, a white body bag for a dead napoleon.

The room still had the same physical points, the usual four walls. One wall was a bank of parallelograms crowned with leaded glass, the diamonds now bowled out with age, a wad of Christmas wrapping stuffed into a missing pane.

The second wall was French doors that once led into the living room. Now the doors were permanently closed. Each pane was covered with salmon and purple swirls of marbled paper. She liked to think she lived within the corners of an expensively bound diary.

A cup rim ran across the upper midsection of the other two walls. Once her cup collection was housed there. That is, until the pet indigo snake reptiled his way between the wall and cups. With each curve of his satanic tail, the cups and saucers toppled. The resulting tones delicately filled the house as Limoges, Royal Doulton, Spode, and Nissan cracked expensively on the hardwood floor.

The snake survived. She had looked at the brilliant shards; then at the snake and felt lucky. She never had to hostess another lady tea because she was the only lady on the block who had enough cups. Nor did she ever have to pack them up again and haul them over to a less-endowed lady's revel. She had lost her cups.

Now she placed her things there, the things she liked to keep, never look at unless to use as a mile marker if any visitor would care to journey through the spoils of her years.

Two squint-eyed newborns sleep in a double frame. Printed hurriedly across the photo are the words "boy," a note on the hour, minutes, poundage, and length. Her babies. Her boys.

Hung by a utility string on a golden tack is a small gathering of dried red roses, upside down, unopened clots of blood.

The ledge holds lines of rocks: volcanics, not the measured stones of sedimentary time nor the heavy lumps of metamorphic eons. But pumice, basalt, lavas, tuffs, tephras, scoria found in the Cascade Mountains, sisters to other rocks she had carefully placed on the trails, a promise testifying to her future return, when she herself was a bundle of bones, ghost of the Cascade Crest, Wonder of the Wonderland Trail.

She was ready. Her calves still had the V worked into the back muscle. Her boots and backpack were vintage Eddie Bauer, and her binocs were definitely REI when REI was still up the stairs on Pike Street before Pike Street went whore.

On her ledge she had an all-day sucker. She licked it just enough to keep it dust free. That sucker had two more years, she imagined.

Then books, lines of books. She had spent hours at used book stores repossessing her favorite books: *Seaweeds at Ebb Tide, Tibetan Book of the Dead, Septic Field Practises, Childbirth by Lamaze, Joy of Sex* with its antidotes *Vile Bodies* and *The Principles and Practise of Sex Therapy*. Next in this display came the *Bible* in the right translation, *Options in Rhetoric, Least You Have to Know About English, Tales of a Fourth Grade Nothing, Upward and Onward in the Garden, Pigtail Days in Old Seattle, Where the Wild Things Are, Edible Incredible,* and *Good Night Moon.* And more.

She had plans to reread these favorites, working up slowly to her favorite passages. But she thought perhaps she didn't have that much reading time left to her. So she began to copy out her favorite passages longhand. She became impatient. So she tore out her favorite pages and kept them in piles next to her reading chair.

Her reading chair was an overstuffed number, The Crotch she called it. Warm, enfolding, it had interesting recesses.

She read there. She never read in bed. If she did, she would have stayed in bed all day, and it was depressing to be in bed all day unwashed, undressed, unbrushed while absorbing the adventures, physical, mental, sexual, of other people. Her vicarious joys were taken easier sitting upright, her teeth flossed, her hair brushed out and caught in a loose grey bun, and her cheeks scrubbed pink.

She had one tea cup. The balique reminded her of her own skin now: fragile, bumpy, the light caught and preserved in the milky whiteness.

She drank Earl Grey tea each morning. She would walk out on the porch, squint into the Seattle weather, and list up her day. Students would leap past her; she would sip and decide.

On her ledge was also a wine goblet. Waterford. Heavy, not appropriate for a white. She called this piece her portable decadence. Occasionally she would catapult and sign up for a Golden Age bus tour when their destination was the Chateau Ste. Michelle Winery.

She would pack her goblet, grab a seat behind the driver. She found his uniform, albeit pure polyester, spruced him up for a conversation. Upon arrival at the carefully placed lawns and token grapevines, she departed the bus and briskly went forward, kicking geese when necessary. She would ascend past the pond, enter through the tour's exit gate, bustle up to the sipping counter, pull out her Waterford, place its sparkling lip under a fine red, perhaps a Cabernet Sauvignon '79, expectable but trusty. She would raise her eyes to meet the eyes of the once-surprised tour guide, words of wine flowing from his lips. As he continued to list out the dead animals that should accompany the various wines, she would say in an undertone to the guide: "Fill it. I've come a long way." Then she would take her goblet, leave the fumes of the casks and tourists, exit the building to emerge among the greens, the bedding flowers, and wet smells of the Sammamish Slough, to take in the weather and to sip well.

Next on her ledge were five bayberry candles, numerous stubs of Advent candles, and two baptismal tapers. The tapers she associated with limbo which the Pope had lately cancelled in spite of generations of dead babies having been cast there unbaptised. The Advent's purples and pinks reminded her of the children's snickers as *Oh Come, Oh Come, Emmanuel* was seasonally rendered off key. The bayberry reminded her of Christmas at Frederick and Nelson when the perfect egg salad san and white clam chowder and Frango mint shake were served on real crockery and the sundae had hot caramel gooped all over the top, not served in a plastic thimble on the side.

Her bed was double, not a queen nor a king nor a waterbed. She had a double bed for herself to wander over feeling for cool places on hot nights, dry places on damp nights, unlumpy spots on restless nights.

She had a bad mattress: hollows, ridges, ravines. But she accommodated them. She curled her body around them, moved about as age and pressure moved them about the geography of her bed. She had done the same for men most of her life, moved herself about the bed for them.

She had only one lover now. He was eighty, a bone to be sure. He came to town twice a year. "Stay over at her place," he'd say. He never said he came "to sleep with her" or said "to crash at her pad," but said "stay over" as if she had the farm down a long road, a big porch, a few chickens and fresh eggs in the evening of his journey through the hen houses of this world.

With her, this was okay. She didn't so much like him, as like the night with him. This visit was a review for her. She had breasts, and thighs, and lips, and a vagina. He had all his spare parts, she knew. He never considered them spare. She did. A luxury like a spare bedroom in good times. Or a spare tire in bad times. Sparity had virtue.

Obviously when she thought about his parts, or more precisely, his part, she was ambiguous in attitude. The night was a review. He did well. She did well. But they both looked past the right cheek of each other and gazed into the kettle of their sexuality in the pattern on the pillow or the pattern on the ceiling depending on who had the most energy or ascendancy that night.

The door from her room went directly into the kitchen, a common kitchen for the boarders. She used the kitchen often. On the kitchen wall was a duty chart. "Deep Cleaning" it said in block letters. The tenants' names were listed in the right hand column. The duties, in multiple listings over the face of the chart, were listed by area: porch, hall, steps, bathroom, laundry room, garbage bins.

She liked deep cleaning: grey beards of mildew in the wizened cheeks of orange peels, tufts and tufts of baby-soft lint, forgotten umbrellas, fly specks, and in the bottom of the shower stall, pubic hairs, black, glossy, kinked.

She left her room and went on campus every day. Under the deciduous trees of fraternity row, she accommodated the irregularities of the root-tortured sidewalk; she ignored the spring running of the sap in the form of chug contests, sorority serenades, posing and flashing. She'd hit campus with enthusiasm.

One day the lecturer in Kane Hall concentrated on the edges of dark holes. She preferred the dissertation defenses in Johnson Hall. Memorable was the paper entitled *Hydrothermal Alteration within Mt. Rainier, Washington*. The ordeal was followed by champagne. The poker game in the English Lounge in Padelford Hall provided an occasional witty aside. Imogen Cunningham's photos at the Henry Art Gallery were a mistake for her. They gave her cataracts. End-of-the-quarter departmental potlucks were tasty. Fisheries had great casseroles and engineering had excellent desserts.

The open air ministers on the greens gave her pause. She also wanted to raise her voice as witness. But she didn't. She adjusted her straw hat, picked lint from her gaberdine coat, then flapped away in her flip flops before her urge to orate became too strong, before the need to recite from *Cat's Cradle* became too deadening. As she moved away from the righteous, she would merely throw back her head and crow in delight.

Her last stop was the Burke Museum, the museum of totem poles, of Northwest mammoths, of butterflies stretched cheaply across styrofoam. Inside she'd pause to look at her favorites. The welcoming totem, two stories high, had pendulous tits hanging down to the statue's waist level. The bottom plane of each breast had a carven face: a muskrat or a beaver, features in red and black. She had to turn her head and bend over to see the humor. She thought the breasts hilarious.

At this museum she'd always use the women's room whether nature called or not for on the way to the room was a reclining Greek male, a token wound in his lovely side. As she would pass by her dying warrior, she would raise her left hand on the way in and her right hand on the way out and briefly caress, only in passing, the cool scrotum of the statue.

Then she would attend the Boiserie, the museum coffee shop. The table and chairs here had arrived from modernized areas of campus as old-fashioned rejects. The tables were wood and heavy; the chairs large and comfortable. The walls of the coffee shop were a nut brown, their golden veneer peeled from a French hunting lodge and reglued here on the wall of this Northwest museum.

The music was insistently baroque. The coffee was French Roast. Expensive. Each day she ordered a cup. Each day they gave her a cup. And then she forgot to pay.

The coffee made her heart buzz, numbed her tongue, while the harpsichord made her fingers tingle, the bass her tongue throb. The chords thundered across her bones until the tears coursed down the scabland of her face like a spring rill on its rush out on dry dirt.

On her centennial birthday she would also come here, let them treat her to a coffee. But instead of egressing through the erratics and columnar basalt of the courtyard, she would return to the circle of totem poles, adzed from red cedar, potlatch images stretched up into the grey of the Northwest sky. She would place herself next to raven, bear, salmon, beaver, and whale. Also in her circle would be the poles of elongated human figures, raised high on occasion as ridiculers or greeters. In this company she, too, would stretch her legs, expand her chest, and lift her arms straight up in wild greeting, her mouth caught in a bellow of welcome.

*M. ANN SPIERS*
*Vol. 9#2&3, 1986*

*"Fringie" refers to someone who lived on the fringe of Seattle's University District during the early sixties.*

## SONG/FOR SANNA

*...in this way the future enters
into us, in order to transform itself
in us before it happens.*
R. M. Rilke

What hasn't happened
intrudes, so much
hasn't yet happened. In the steamy

kitchens we meet in, kettles
are always boiling, water for tea, the steep
infusions we occupy
hands and mouth with, steam
filming our breath, a convenient

subterfuge, a disguise
for the now
sharp intake, the measured
outlet of air, the sigh, the gutting
loneliness

of the present where
what hasn't happened will
not be ignored, intrudes, separates
from the conversation like milk
from cream, desire

rising between the cups, brimming
over our saucers, clouding the minty
air, its own
aroma a pungent
stress, once again, you will get
up, put on your coat, go

home to the safer passions, moisture
clinging still to your spoon, as the afternoon
wears on, and I miss, I
miss you.

*OLGA BROUMAS*
*Vol. 1#1, 1976*

## TO PRAISE

I want to praise bodies
nerves and synapses
the shudder that travels the spine
    like fish darting

I want to praise the mouth
that warm wet lair where the tongue reclines
and the tongue, roused
    slithering a cool path

I want to praise hands
those architects that create us anew
fingers, cartographers, revealing
    who we can become
and palms, cupped priestesses
    worshipping the long slow curve

I want to praise muscle
and the heart, that flamboyant champion
    with its insistent pelting like
    tropical rain, fierce and fast

I want to praise hair
the sweep of it, a breeze, over skin
utter softness under the soles

and feet, arch taut
    stretching like cats

I want to praise the face, engraved
like a river bed, open
a surprise, like laughter

breasts, cornucopia
nipples that jump up, gleeful
    like a child greeting the day

and clitoris, shimmering
a huge tender pearl
    in that succulent oyster

I want to praise the love cries
sharp, brilliant as ice
and the roar that swells in the lungs
    like an avalanche

I want to praise the gush, the hot
spring thaw of it, the rivers
    wild with it

Bodies, our extravagant bodies

And I want to praise you, how you have
lavished yours
upon mine
    until I want to praise

*ELLEN BASS*
*Vol. 8#1, 1983*

## AUBADE II

Sometimes, when you're asleep, I want to do
it to myself while I'm watching you. It
would be easy, two fingers along my clit,
back, in, back out. Your skin's heat comes into
me, adjacent. Through the mussed chrysanthemum-
petals, your big child's sleep-face, closed around
its openness, gives me your mouth to ground
on, but only with my eyes. I could come
like that, but I don't—take you against your will,
it seems like, and I wouldn't; rather wait
adrowse in sunlight, with this morning heat
condensing, a soft cloud above my groin
gently diffusing brightness there, until
you wake up, and you bring it down like rain.

*MARILYN HACKER*
*Vol. 10#1, 1986*

## SONNET ON A NEW BED

We'll write one by hand:
Rhyme of my arcing fingers with
the drawn bow of your thigh,
assonance of tongues traversing
the same dark slippery places,
the echo of our faces and
the firm exacting diction of your hand
stroke for strophe sure
as the measured march of metric feet—
iamb, iamb, I am pentameter;

passion written on a linen sheet
taut as any sonnet. Fourteen lines
to sound the strong and ready beat
of love held tight by corner rhymes.

*REBECCA GORDON*
*Vol. 3#2, 1978*

## TWO IOWA FARMERS

We know each other too long
make love like two Iowa farmers
in plaid flannel nightgowns—
He gets on top
licks a flame in her
then can't keep it up
His big thing
withered to a worm in rain

She's large under warm covers
Half wanting it
half wanting sleep
in a mouth that doesn't bother
with lipstick
He reaches down
like it was molasses puddin'
Moves her mound of dry hay
She rocks her eyes back
dreams of berries
goosedown
tar poured in the feeding station
She winds up heaving like windmills
Station wagon come to a stop
He pulls out the key
She's done for
but has some duty still
in her blind body

He mounts
this time for himself
for his rows of sweet corn
the tractor
for the old wood barn
He's movin' with it all
It's hard through thick mud
His heart's pounding
   huge flights of birds
   lift their autumn wings
He arches his neck like a dog's
full moon night
Then takes a nose dive like a paper plane
It's all over
What he was doin' anyhow
Finds this warm body
like thick cream
snorin' under him
He wonders:
Only Iowa!
could make it this good.

NATALIE GOLDBERG
*Vol. 4#2, 1979*

COMING TOGETHER

I want to do it in different rooms
I want us to turn out all the lights
even in the heavens
one by one twist those bulbs too
and after traveling up there in the atmosphere
come down to the living room
on a pale blue blanket
Drink beer
till we become shimmering
clicking clear glasses together
and with the pure light of our own
tell stories in the naked heat of summer
Us two violets of this worn out marriage

When I first met you
I thought you were water
sounds traveling down the body
Let's sing such silences
in the motion, I imagine, of elephants
making love in the African sky
or whales rising
out of the center of the Atlantic
coming together on the surface of water
or ants
hundreds of us covering one square of sidewalk
carrying each other over to the grass
Even more joyous
like cokes on a counter in Nebraska
or the stove and refrigerator wanting each other
all day across the kitchen
The ceiling
wings outspread
longing for the floor

I want you in all these ways
then direct as ketchup dropped from the bottle
onto hot steak
or the finger touching ice cubes
Right through our spines and out our teeth
with lungs in full sail
and our chests rising and falling like mountains

*NATALIE GOLDBERG*
*Vol. 7#3, 1983*

AMAZON TWINS

I.

You wanted to compare, and there
we were, eyes on each eye, the lower
lids
squinting
suddenly awake

though the light was dim. Looking away
some time ago, you'd said
   *the eyes are live*
   *animals, domiciled in our head*
but more than the head

is crustacean-like. Marine
eyes, marine
odors. Everything live
(tongue, clitoris, lip and lip)
swells in its moist shell. I remember the light

warped round our bodies finally
crustal, striated with sweat.

II.

In the gazebo-like cafe, you gave
me food from your plate, alert
to my blood sweet hungers
double-edged
in the glare of the sun's
and our own
twin heat. Yes, there

we were, breasts on each side, Amazons
adolescent at twentynine
privileged
to keep the bulbs and to feel the blade
swell, breath-sharp
on either side. In that public place

in that public place.

*OLGA BROUMAS*
*Vol. 1#1, 1976*

●

RISKS:

When your hair beats over me like gold
& sweeps me like brooms of Demeter

& your mouth burns my waist into forgetting

& your fingers wet my hips
with words for the opening of caves

& your tongue finds my invisible vein of salt

& your breasts fall on mine like the night canopy

& your eyes stand awake like sailors

& you rock me like a hammock
under the near stars

*JOAN LARKIN*
*Vol. 8#1, 1983*

Untitled

*silver print*
*8" x 10"*
Vol. 8#2, 1984

*SILVIA SANTAL*

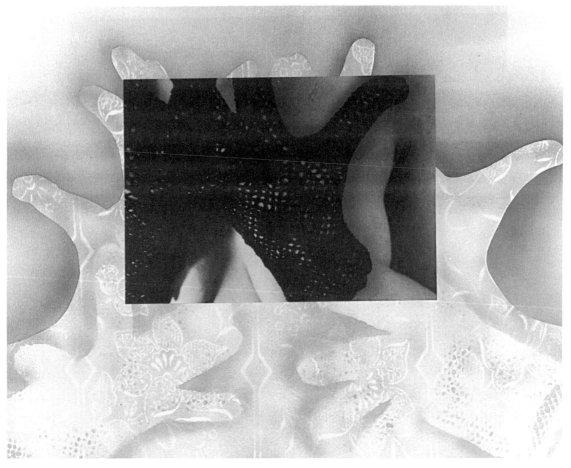

*Grandmother's Gloves II*      *color photograph with airbrush*      MEREDITH JENKINS
*16" x 16"*
*Vol. 6#2, 1982*

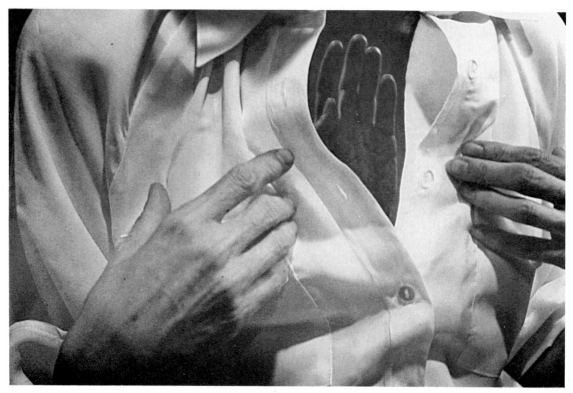

Untitled                    *black and white photograph*                    LINDA JOAN MILLER
                                    *Vol. 8#1, 1983*

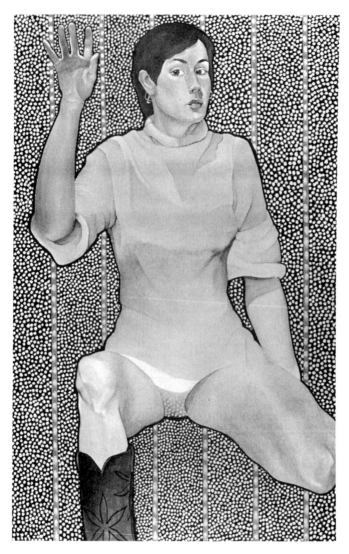

*Self-Portrait as Mary Martin*     SANDRA McKEE
*as Peter Pan*                *oil*
                         *36" x 36"*
                      *Vol. 2#3, 1978*

*Shining Woman #11 (Amber)*      *acrylic*      FAEDRA KOSH
                                 *36" x 42"*
                                 *Vol. 8#3, 1984*

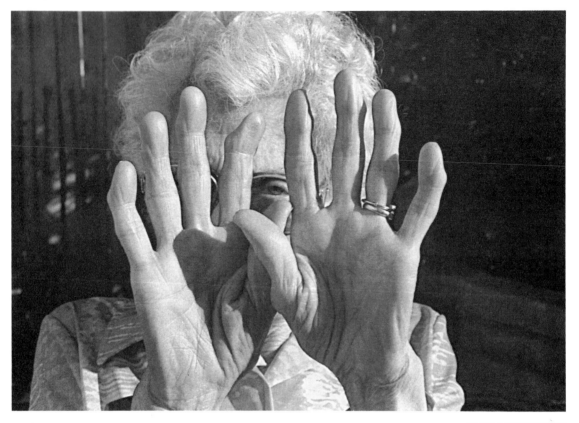

*Tushu*                     *black and white photograph*                     ANN MEREDITH
                            *Vol. 9#2&3, 1986*

*Beginning "Women a New Myth"*      *JANET CULBERTSON*
*ink and charcoal*
*40" x 60"*
*Vol. 4#3, 1980*

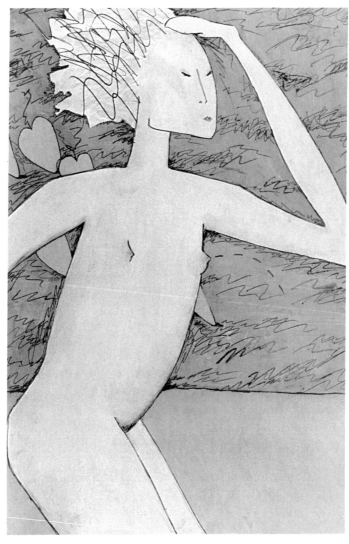

SP#1                 *DANA LEIGH SQUIRES*
*enamel and oil pastels on paper*
*24" x 36"*
*Vol. 6#1, 1981*
photo by Kristine Larsen

*Demi Tut Cups, Pyramid Teapot*          *earthenware*          RONNA NEUENSCHWANDER
                                              *10" high*
                                          *Vol. 5#1, 1980*
                                          photo by David Reinert

*Hawaiian Shirt & Dicko's Skirt*     *oil on canvas*     LIZA *von* ROSENSTIEL
                                      *72" x 72"*
                                      *Vol. 10#1, 1986*

*O*n mountaintops, in deserts, in polluted urban areas, flowers bloom. The cycle is determined by the sun, the moon, and the seasons. The plant, with an innate ability, tracks the life-giving path of the sun, its leaves and flowers turning always towards the sun's warmth.

One of woman's greatest sources of power is her connection to the cyclical nature of life. Women's bodies are regulated by blood, sea, and moon—forces outside our control. This allows an understanding of the dark as a part of the whole. In this section women dismantle myths, struggle with mortality, and celebrate moments of grace and transformation when the darkness is illuminated.

## YOU WANT ME WHITE

You want me pure,
You want me made of froth,
Made of mother-of-pearl.
I should be a lily
Above all, chaste.
Of tenuous perfume.
Corolla closed.

Not even a ray of the moon
Should have penetrated me.
Nor a daisy
Call herself my sister.
You want me like the snow,
You want me white,
You want me pure.

You who have
Drunk from every cup,
Your lips stained
With fruit and honey.
You who have abandoned your flesh
Celebrating Bacchus
At vine-covered tables.
You who in the
Black gardens of deceit
Dressed in red
Rushed to corruption.

You who still have
Your skeleton intact
I don't know
Through what miracle,
You want me white
(God forgive you)
You want me chaste
(God forgive you)
You want me pure!

Flee to the woods;
Get yourself to the mountain;
Clean your mouth;
Live in huts;
Touch the damp earth
With your hands;
Nourish your body
With bitter roots;
Drink from the rocks;
Sleep on the frost;
Renew your tissue
With salt and water;
Speak to the birds
And rise at dawn.
And when your flesh
Is returned to you,
And when you have put
Back into it the soul
You've left around
In bedrooms,
Then, my good man,
Ask that I be white,
Ask that I be like the snow,
Ask that I be chaste.

*ALFONSINA STORNI*
translated by *ALMITRA DAVID*
*Vol. 5#2&3, 1980*

REAL VANILLA

Fifty Portuguese sailors
in uniform
in one tight railway car
(with all their baggage)
They lift small fish like smelt
holding them high by the tail
and eat them headfirst
in unison.
We are passing close to the sea. If trains in progress
did not shudder and roar, we could hear the
smacking applause barnacles make at sunset
after the tide
goes out
like fifty Portuguese sailors.
The way the friend of your friend smacked
in the cafe outside Madrid. My,
what big teeth you
American girls have
when you smile,
if you only would.
I exchanged glances with
the fish on the table, cocking my head like a robin,
my left eye to the left orb of the fish.
On my right now, one Portuguese sailor,
and one on my left, fish eyes
disappearing into mouths, a rhythm of winks.
The rails pass beside mountains,
sun laying a thick haze, making the snow
soft and vanilla, slightly yellow like Real
Vanilla ice cream. I remember somebody told me once
they put fish parts, oil or something from the ground bones maybe,
in fake vanilla ice cream. Must be the small white bones
and that's why it's not vanilla yellow.
My brother always ate real vanilla.
I ate chocolate.

I have never eaten the head of a fish.
Whether or not oysters have heads
is a technicality.
I have eaten whole oysters,
but never raw.
I did not eat any of the fish on the table
in the cafe
outside Madrid.
A fish with its left eye on my fork,
the friend of your friend with both eyes on my . . .

Fifty Portuguese sailors with twice
as many eyes and lips,
an endless smack of fish, smaller than smelt,
headfirst
in unison.

*SIBYL JAMES*
*Vol. 4#3, 1980*

## AGAINST CINDERELLA

I can't believe it.
Whoever made it up is pulling my foot
so it'll fit that shoe.
I'll go along with martyrdom:
she swept and wept; she mended, stoked the fire,
slaved while her three stepsisters,
who just happened to oblige their meanness
by being ugly, dressed themselves.
I'll swallow that there was a Singer godmother,
who magically could sew a pattern up
and hem it in an hour,
that Cinderella got to be a debutante
and lost her head and later lost her shoe.
But there I stop.
I can't believe
that no one but one woman in that town
had that size foot, could fit into that shoe.
I've felt enough of lost and found
to know that if you lose your heart
to anyone you've crowned into a prince,
you might not get it back;
that the old kerchief trick,
whether you drop a shoe, your clothes, your life,
doesn't do much but litter up the world.
That when the knock at last comes to your door,
you might not be home or bothered.
That some of us have learned to go barefoot
knowing the mate to one foot is the other.

*JULIA ALVAREZ*
*Vol. 7#1, 1982*

# I LISTEN TO ALICE WALKER
# ON A POCKET RADIO

Sitting at my desk, I concentrate
on a distant voice through static,
the radio pressed to my ear,
antenna full-length.

I hear Alice Walker tell about
earthquakes,
her mama's roots and seeds,
aunts who shed their weekday uniforms
            for Saturday's perfume and furs,
        turning (right before her girl-eyes)
                into fragrant, velvety blossoms.

I press the small speaker closer
to hear her voice
tell how we all require
the wonder of transformations,

and a black, silver-stamened flower
unfolds at my ear.

*PAULANN PETERSEN*
*Vol. 9#1, 1985*

# LEARNING TO SWIM AT FORTY-FIVE

*I could not whistle and walk in*
*storms along Lake Michigan's shore*
*...I could not swallow the lake*
Clarence Major

Having given up hope for a high wire act
I've taken to water and the quicksilver
Danger of working words hand over hand.
At the edge of the pool I am locked in gravity
And remember the jeers at Girl Scout camp
Where *catfish* meant anyone who lived in a ghetto
With no pools and no need to tan and everyone
Spent more time learning how to keep their hair
From *going bad* than they did learning breast strokes.

And yes Clarence, I learned to swallow the lake
Including all that it held and what I was told
By Mrs. Fitzsimmons of Harris Stowe Teachers
Who later said I couldn't hold the elements
Of tone or the way words break and run like rain,
The *Hecates* and *Africs* filling the page
Until it grows buoyant under the weight of sonnets,
A feat she believed so unconsciously automatic
It arrived full blown at birth.

For forty years I've lived under the pull of air,
All the while knowing survival meant learning
To swim in strange waters. *Just jump in and do it*
They yelled at camp, then tossed me heels over head
Their humor an anchor dragging me down.
There I defied training films and descended just once,
My body stone weight and full of the first primal fear
Of uncurling from the water belly of a mother country.
There I could not whistle in the face of the storm
And even my legs were foreign.

*Poetry like swimming can not be learned*
Fitzsimmons insisted as I rubbed the smooth skin
Behind my ears where gill flaps had failed to appear.
Now years later, I voluntarily step below the surface
And there beneath the chlorine blue, I am finally reptilian
And so close to the Middle Passage, I will pay any price
For air. If silence has a smell, it is here
Where my breath fizzles in a champagne of its own making,
Where I must learn to sing to the rhythms of water
The strange currents and patterns of moons and tides.

Fitzsimmons, it doesn't happen all at once. To swim
You must learn to labor under the threat of air lost
Forever and hold fear close to you like a safety net.
You must imagine the body, the way it floats and extends
First like an anchor, then a lizard or a dead leaf,
Direction is some point where the sun is inverted and sweet
Air hammers the brain with signals that must be ignored.
You learn to take risks, to spread yourself thin,
You learn to look *through a glass darkly*
And in your darkness, build elegies of your own rhythms,
And yes Fitzsimmons, you learn when to swallow
The lake and when to hold to the swell of it.

COLLEEN J. McELROY
*Vol. 7#2, 1982*

# THE SEASON OF BITTER ROOT AND SNAKE VENOM

It is the season of bitter root and snake venom,
the season when the children vanish,
returning as adults (their dreams tumbling
out of suitcases they re-pack and take with them,
my home a pit-stop on their way to newer stars),
familiar strangers whose child-faces
they have eaten up whole, small traces of the old lustre
but the children are gone. And it is the season
of the dying parent, strapped to a bed,
shouting obscenities, staring at me with white eyes
when I say "Papa" and he replies, "I don't understand."
The season of the 120° flash, a rock wall
surrounding me with blasts of heat
that coils into a steamroller
and mows me down. Panting I lie in the pit
of this rock valley, my rescuer a witch
of the hidden moon who offers herbs. I open my dry mouth
to sip and chew her bitter root and snake venom.
Slithering into a shady crevice in the rock
I survey the valley, the mountain peak.
I survey and I sip and I chew.
And I learn how to hiss.

*PESHA GERTLER*
*Vol. 9#2&3, 1986*

## BRUJA: WITCH

I wait for the owl.
I wait for Tuesday and Thursday nights
to leave my slow body, to fly.

Beneath white moonlight
I lie on the hard desert.
I close my eyes, slow my heart,
pull my life in, breathe it out
into the owl's warm feathers.

I stretch into the long free wings,
feel the air gently hold me.
Gliding above my adobe home I see
my wrinkled, gray-haired body
still, far below.

The owl and I are one.
With large gold eyes
I spy my victims. Through a dirty
window I see two nude bodies trying
to escape into each other.

I laugh and call from a nearby tree,
"Amigo, who is that woman?
Not your wife, eh? You don't taste
your wife like that. Let us see.
Our whole village wants to watch."
I laugh again.

Then I fly into the night.
My work is done. A frightened husband
will run to the wife who paid me
three American dollars.

I am free
until the rooster's song plunges me
down into my tired bones.
I tilt and dip and soar.
I smell mesquite. Beneath white
stars, I dance.

*PAT MORA*
*Vol. 8#2, 1984*

## LA REVOLUCIÓN ES UNA CHAVALA DE CINCO AÑOS*

You understand, she says, that if
I die it doesn't matter, someone will
come after me to love this revolution

the way that any one of us
loves the cranky little girl
who wanders through the meeting while
we discuss what's serious:
how to move the beans and rice

from market to barrio, and if
the price supports will last
and who will take the last round
watching in the warm dark street
tonight. It's not always

her mother who scoops her
up from the dirt, who swings
a gun off a shoulder to make
a place for her, not always
her mother who pulls straight

the little shirt, pinned and
sewn together with coarse thread,
who swings her toward the rafters
overhead and holds her upside-
down for one great, giddy

moment, sets her on the ground,
a barefoot sun in dungarees. Any
one of us would do these things.

She smiles dark in army green,
rests a rifle on her parted knees
talks about an easy death in battle
while a little girl careens,

explodes in cheap pink nylon
around the cardboard room, settles
in the sergeant's olive arms
like some bright hibiscus bloom.

*REBECCA GORDON*
*Vol. 9#1, 1985*

*The Revolution is like a five-year-old girl*—Nicaraguan saying.

A CALL TO GRACE                                    *ANDREA CARLISLE*

*For Linda Belen*

For a long time before dawn Miller lay in bed next to his sleeping wife, listening as the sprinkling of rain on the rooftop lightened. He was pleased. Perhaps it was finally letting up. Although the rain was usually all right with him, it was April now and he, like most people in Oregon, had become weary of the opaque blanket of sky pulled over the landscape. It frustrated him to look up and see lingering mists and fogs covering the lush green shoulders of surrounding hills. Enough! He wanted spring. It was not satisfying that the gray light of the lengthening days expanded little by little. He wanted the clear light of sunshine.

Miller was an old man and quiet. He tried to be patient too, but his body grew more restless night after night and he could barely sleep at all. Awake in the night's blue shadows his toes wiggled, his heart beat noisily, this muscle or that muscle twitched. To occupy himself he squinted to trace the bones of his bedroom ceiling. He and his son, Ian, had built the house. He thought of Ian climbing around in the sky with him, making the rooftop. Both strong and brown in the sun. They worked steadily, with a kind of grim determination, Miller thought now. Where was the joy? The pride? How many houses had they ever built, for heaven's sake? Now Ian was gone, living in an east coast city, selling insurance. Miller sighed. His eyes glazed, refocused, glazed again.

Sleep did not return and he didn't want it to. He wanted to stay awake so if the sun did come he could rise to meet it. He could jump up at the first ray and rush out into the morning, run like a child, although he knew that was impossible. Still, it was what his legs wanted, and his heart. Remembering the Dakota prairie sixty years before, he saw again the high yellow grass, the gopher holes, two bull snakes hanging from a tree by a creek, saw himself shivering at night under a patchwork quilt when coyotes howled into the cold black sky.

His life was a set of these pictures now. He did not attach feelings to them, but decided getting old must mean this kind of distanced review. Sometimes he saw Ian growing up again as though he were watching a movie, or saw his own father milking a cow and squirting the warm milk into his mouth, and then in the next frame came Ian and Belle, Miller's wife, getting into the old blue Ford that would take them from the Dakotas to Oregon with him.

The pictures did not come in any special order. Sometimes there were three or four or a dozen of them pertaining to a nearly forgotten subject. In this last series, for example, he saw the three of them leaving with much excitement and then enjoying their journey. Every mood of the great western sky was worthy of exclamation. Miller thought that Ian had kept them both fully alive then. Look at this! Look at that! He was irresistible. After the boy grew up and went to college, Miller and Belle had very little energy of their own for looking at new things, and what their son had given them slowly dribbled away. It was renewed on his school vacations, but then he was married and truly gone and Miller's own marriage had slowly rusted in the steady Oregon rain.

Pictures continued drifting by, eyes closed or open, some in order, some not—his hand touching his father's rough red fingers, Ian riding his first bicycle, Belle cooking dinners. His life was this long movie now, he thought, one dead picture after another. He wanted to break out of it, but into what? He didn't know. All he had was this body, this life.

The best he could hope for was spring. The years had added up but without much reward. There was a thinness about those years, a watery quality. He thought getting older meant that the core within him that he sensed was there, was truly himself, became discovered and known, that a solidness came with passing years that could be felt and offered. Instead he had put his life together without much thought as to how to create this and it didn't seem to come on its own. He found himself unable to even talk to anyone about his life or thoughts, or even about the weather, not his deepest feelings about the weather anyway. Certainly he could not share much with Belle, who hardly knew him after all these years and whom he hardly knew except in the sense of familiarity. His muscle had dropped away without even a comment from her, his face grown longer, and his energy slackened without a house to build or a barn or a real farm to take care of. Several months ago he had given up the dozen or so little projects a day that kept him busy and began spending much of his time with an old brown horse he bought at an auction. It was not a horse he purchased for riding, but for companionship. The horse was the only thing he did not make wrong in his life, including himself. Because he wanted to love something completely, the horse was exempt from all his judgments. Its only requirements were to breathe, eat and move.

Belle began to snore. He turned and looked at her. Even in the dark her white face was quite visible, was known to him. In sleep all the lines on her brow and around her mouth melted. Often she turned to him suddenly in the dead of their nights together and whimpered like a frightened animal. He gently whispered her out of the bad dreams without waking her completely, although he knew that when morning came they would put on their rusted masks again and share no more than twenty words until just before supper. At that time Belle did her knitting in a high-backed wooden rocker in the kitchen and gave a running, tiresome account of the neighbors and her day of part-time work at the real estate office in town. Miller's habit was to sit at the table and read the newspaper as she spoke.

Now he lay next to her, looking at her, but thinking about the horse. He wanted spring to come for the horse as much as for himself. The horse was old too and Miller was certain, although he had no veterinary evidence, that the animal's bones ached with the dampness. He liked to go to the barn first thing to feed it.

"You and that darned horse!" Belle liked to say as he shuffled out the back door. "Can't you eat some breakfast yourself first?"

He preferred to take an apple for each of them.

He wondered again at the rain. It was never a single sound but many small sounds at once, yet so quiet, so soft. This amazed him. One would think that if someone were up in the sky pouring out water by the billions of buckets, it would make an awful crashing sound, but no. This came of itself and timed itself. It fell perfectly, drop behind drop behind drop, each knowing exactly when to fall. Each waited in line like a little soldier in the eternal assault on the Northwest. And the Northwest, woodsy, dense and submissive, swallowed it all.

It was certainly not like the Dakotas where the rain pelted down the dust or soaked the fertile plains and then the sky itself appeared to move off and leave him. He never thought about how rainstorms happened as a prairie child. They came. They went. The earth cherished them.

A set of pictures passed by that made Miller very uncomfortable. There was his father, weeping at the sight of rain and there was Miller, a young boy, holding his hand, a hand that was hard and dry as a corncob left in the sun. He looked up from the horizon darkening with the storm and saw teardrops staining his father's solemn face, falling down his wide, sunburned cheeks, silently. His father, who could make fields flourish at the drop of a few seeds, who dug his own well and called water right out of the earth, who birthed calves, slaughtered beef, constructed buildings, harvested crops, this person was not known to cry. Even when Miller's mother had died, the man had not cried, though Miller's own tears fell freely.

Miller could not bear those silent tears, grateful for rain. He wanted to take his father and run away, snatch him from the boundaries of weather, release him from this humiliation. He knew the rainfall meant survival, but he wanted them both free from the need to survive.

The pictures relentlessly continued. There was the old man looking down at him, seeing his son's fear and disappointment. Immediately the rough hand pulled away. He brushed the tears from his face, then walked off. They never spoke of it and neither cried again in the other's presence, but Miller felt shame at his disappointment, and tried to make up for it, tried to comfort him, tried to quietly keep rescuing his father with his eyes, letting his own face grow sad to keep him company.

His grown intelligence told him that tears were not a crime, that the issue of survival was a mean one. But the part of his mind that held this information straight for him seemed to not be in communication with another part that experienced acute discomfort whenever this memory recurred. Even now he wanted to take his father away, out of that picture.

His movie fluttered ahead ten years and he saw himself driving away from the old man's grave in their blue battered pickup truck. He drove as fast as he could down the country roads. Run! He called internally to his own long-ago image, a tiny figure against the blank horizon, bald earth and pale empty sky. Run away!

He could not hold back and entered the picture, driving the truck down the straight line of gravel road. He did not know where to go. The sky followed him. It formed boulders of clouds above him and growled with thunder. Twisted hands of lightning reached down and grabbed for the earth around him. Fat raindrops blurred visibility through the dirty windshield. Frightened, he managed to pull himself out of the picture and into his bed in Oregon again, into the quiet Oregon rain, a relief after that storm. Oregon, like his marriage, omitted thunder and lightning and surrendered, without fuss, to the inevitability of its partnership with this form of weathering.

Belle began to snore again but caught it midbreath, turned and reached for him, putting her arm across his chest, her knee over his thigh. She breathed warmly near his ear. He very slowly raised his own hand from his side and placed it gently over hers, but even deep in sleep she sensed intimacy, slowly unfolded her body from around him, and turned away.

I cannot sleep, he told himself, and wondered if his son were sleeping. What time was it in Baltimore anyway? He could never remember which way the time went, west to east, slower or faster?

He could not remember because he truly did not want to remember his son at all. What was it to him if Ian slept or paced the floor? He would just as soon forget him. Having a son provided pleasure for twenty years or so then so much for worry and happiness. Let the boy go. Let him call and say this or that and I love you, Dad, but what did it matter really? How could a son shorten the long day now? What good was having a son in Baltimore when the blackberry bushes crept night after night into the garden and snarled back at his morning attacks on them? What good a son against his vast disappointment with life, his silence?

"No, I won't forgive him," he told Belle, as he stared out the window. This statement came from him at least once a month.

"I don't see what you're talking about, Miller," she always replied. "What's there to forgive him for?"

He could not look at her at those times. Her honestly confused face disturbed him. She was clearly puzzled and anxious when it seemed so simple to him. After all, he had stayed with his own father long after his mother died, and he did not leave until the man was dead and buried.

"I didn't leave until Papa was dead and in the ground," he said righteously to himself.

"But then you ran like a man possessed," a voice said back.

This stopped his inner conversation. He couldn't tell Belle anything about that part of his life. He excused himself from talking to her by telling himself she didn't need to know every blessed thing about him. He loved her but had never intended to live this long into his life with just her. She was too cold, too distant. He wanted a family around him, a son, grandchildren. That was the way it was supposed to be. Kindly old grandpa with his young family around him. Who ever thought the boy would up and move to the East Coast? Why the devil had he gone and left him with just her and a past that ran on and on like an endless TV rerun?

"No, I can't forgive him," he would say, catching his reflection in the window, his long face, glasses sliding down his nose revealing watery gray eyes, brown hat pulled down and nearly covering the wings of fluffy white hair around the tops of his ears.

Then he knew enough, before she pressed him, to walk away and go down to visit the horse or go fight the blackberries. He could never say to her no, this is not what I want, just being with you. This is not what I planned at all.

"I'm morbid," he whispered into the shadows of the bedroom, passing judgment on his thoughts, and determined something cheerier. Again the horse came to mind. He wanted to feel its warm breath against his cheek, pat the thick musty winter coat, and hear the playful swish of tail like a spray of light rain blown against a window. He liked the pleasing hollow clap of hoof on the wooden barn floor. Everything about the horse pleased him.

An instant later he was pleased about something else. The rain, he noted, had indeed ended. He rose quietly and looked outside. Yes, dawn soon. He put on a flannel shirt and overalls, then sat in a chair by the window, with one of Belle's endless supply of afghans around his shoulders to keep off the chill.

He fought sleep but drifted, dreamed and started. In an hour he opened his eyes onto the sun rising, burning white and pink around the edges of Mt. Hood to the east. Just as it popped over the summit, he gave a gasp of pleasure.

Belle woke. "What is it, Miller?"

"It's spring," he said. He felt like a child caught at something and wanted to rush off. "I'm going out."

He stood up.

"How long have you been awake, sitting there?" She was incredulous.

"I'm going out to the horse," he said.

"Figures," she grunted, and rolled over.

The horse waited in the barn just beyond the backyard. The barn stood at the edge of a pasture fringed by a forest.

In the kitchen Miller put on his red and black plaid jacket and his old brown hat, all the while looking out the window at the sun filling up his yard, a wide stretch of wild growth, ferns and weeds and grasses determined to grow every shade of green and cover every inch of earth with as much life as possible. Fully dressed, he washed his face and hands. He was more anxious to get out to the land than he had thought. He wanted to roam over every part of it. There were just over twenty acres now. Once there had been one hundred, but Belle had sold it through her real estate office, parcel by parcel.

"We don't need it," she said, and he couldn't argue. He did not farm anymore. They didn't need money, but others could use the land. At first he felt as though pieces of his body were being cut off as she sold this few acres or that, and that he had been reduced to a mere gentleman's acreage. He complained repeatedly, but after awhile grew comfortable with it. The size of the place especially suited him and the horse. They could see what they owned in a single day. Miller did not tell Belle that he had become satisfied because he didn't know how to change himself in front of her. So he said nothing and hoped she knew it was all right.

He suspected she was still awake and waited for him to go outside before she got up. The horse waited, too. He felt joyful as he opened the door and stepped into a crisp air and the expanding light.

The forest beyond the barn was still dark, but the sun threw light over the yard and the pasture. He paused to look at drops of water clinging to the rosebush near the back door. There was the light of the sun imprisoned in the delicate globes of rain, prisms of pink, yellow, green, blue and violet, light that would disappear as soon as the drop fell. He looked out at the pasture. The high grasses and weeds shimmered, newly washed and golden. Miller knew it was impossible, but he could swear the earth smelled different on this sunny day; not with the heat of the sun, for it was early still and the air raw and cold, but the day itself smelled different, like newborn kittens.

He paused only once, pretending to kneel and tie his boot, but actually glanced back quickly at the house. She was not coming. No sound came from that direction.

There were days when she followed him. He pretended not to know. Neither ever mentioned it, but he felt her there. He and the horse always walked a curving route through the pasture, his feet on a path, the horse beside him, its long legs and belly swishing in the high wet grass. She followed at a distance, not too often. He might have looked back, but he didn't. Once he had, and she was startled. He had turned quickly, determined to call to her. He saw her blue and white print dress against the heavy green of the pine trees, but almost as soon as he saw her, she stepped back, then turned around and went quickly, almost running, back toward the house.

He didn't know how to ask her to join them. She didn't know how to make it happen either, so he and the horse always walked on and she stayed behind.

Now and then she worked outside the barn door when he was inside brushing the horse. In the fall she refinished an old chair not too far from them. He could hear her. She could hear him, but they didn't speak.

At Christmas she left two pony-shaped cookies for him and the horse on a paper plate covered with aluminum foil and a green bow stuck on top. She put them just inside the door of the barn, but he had not mentioned it when he returned to the house. He was touched but his voice forgot how to say so, his brain could not remember the words. He opened his mouth several times at her and was frustrated by the silence within him.

Finally she pretended not to notice and whenever his mouth opened again that day, she filled the void quickly with her own words: "You're probably going to say you don't want sweet potatoes. Well, they're very good. Here, try some brown sugar on them." Or, "You probably want to know when Ian's going to call. Well, I don't know. Maybe he can't get through. Maybe all the lines are full, the trunk lines, whatever they're called." Eventually Miller gave up.

The horse called out to him, a rippling octave high to low across the yard.

"I'm comin', boy," he called back. It whinnied again and Miller hastened his step. His black boots glistened in the wet grass.

The mountain and sun and repeated horse's call formed a golden strand that gently tugged at his heart, pulling him eastward into the new life of spring and a certain old and reliable way of being, altogether so powerful that the deep folds of his long face quivered into a smile. He smiled at the barrel of feed standing in the shadow of the barn door, scooped up some oats in a can and walked into the barn itself. Bits of dust danced through a wide island of light falling from an open window. The old brown horse stepped forward and jerked its head up in salute. Its loud greeting echoed up into the rafters.

Miller loved the horse and the horse, he could plainly see, loved him. Whenever he brushed the thick coat, he told the animal his troubles and worries. The horse sighed or shivered or swished its tail and turned to look with deep brown watery sadness into Miller's eyes.

This morning as he reached to pat the horse's neck he said, "Well, whaddya know, pal, it's spring, eh? Finally, my friend, finally!"

He took out their apples from his deep pockets and they each bit into the fruit. Miller sighed and leaned against the animal. "I wisht just once she'd wake up, boy, just once. She'd see her own arms around me and hear herself cryin'. I'd sure be damn lonely without you, fella. I'd rather be dead than be so lonely."

The horse sniffed at the oats so Miller poured them into a bucket nailed to the wall, took a wide brush from the shelf and began to smooth the thick coat.

He brushed, the animal ate, and the barn filled with Miller's dissatisfaction. "Yessir, sometimes I sure do miss that boy of mine. Even when I don't want to." He noticed the horse shifting its weight from one side to the other. It seemed impatient. It would not finish the food but kept raising its head to look at the sun pouring through the window. Hardly a sigh of sympathy at all. In the middle of one of Miller's sentences, the animal shook its head, backed out of the stall, turned and walked out the barn door into the warm light of the morning.

"I'll be," Miller said and stepped outside. This independence was new to him. He had only known the horse through the fall and winter. He did his best to continue the conversation. "So, you like this here springtime, eh fella? Pretty morning. Makes me feel a bit younger myself. Makes me feel like draggin' my old bones around a bit faster than usual. I'll say!"

The horse took a few steps forward and stopped to look at the mountain, the forest, a hawk swooping down over the pasture. The animal seemed completely alert. It watched and listened, then took a few more steps away from Miller, who had never known it to move off by itself like this. He liked to put a lead on it, which he held loosely but which allowed him control nonetheless. He wondered if he had made a mistake, letting it just come out like this. He felt a rush of anxiety.

The horse began to walk quickly toward the gate to the pasture, which stood open. Miller experienced a flash of annoyance. It was not the horse that was supposed to lead him, damn it. He was supposed to lead the horse. That was the game. He went back into the barn and took the leather halter down from its place by the stall. When he came outside again the animal was farther away, through the gate, loping into the pasture.

Miller heard himself give excuses for it. It was spring, after all, and there was a kind of instinct, but the annoyance had all the authority and would not relinquish its hold on Miller's mind. It stuck to his brain like a fly to flypaper.

"Damn it!" he quickened his step and tried to catch up, hoping that Belle was not watching him make a fool of himself from the kitchen window. How ridiculous he would look to her, an old man trotting after an old horse who was by now far ahead and moving with considerable spirit.

"Whoa, fella! Now!" Miller called out, but the horse would not have it. It felt the sun on its back and its nose filled with the sweetness of the new season. It broke loose from old age and habit and kicked its hooves a bit higher than usual as it moved, free from the cold rainfall, the long dark nights, the shadows of the barn.

Warm blood rushed into its heart. A keen thrust of energy, almost burning, jumped through its thighs. Stiffness in the legs melted and, as the blood began to flow through the muscles, the legs moved more quickly. Soon it was trotting across the wide pasture toward the forest where light was beginning to fill the trees. Behind, the old man followed, running now, his face red and raw with anger.

"Come back here!" Miller cried, "You come back!" He raged that he could not call out as loud as he wanted for fear that Belle would hear him and make fun of him, and raged at the thought that he cared and raged at that thought, too. He ran panting, stopped, rested, ran again, but the horse kept going steadily into the distance.

Was he far enough away from her to cry? He could not remember why she mustn't hear him. It hurt too much to think of her, but he could not stop. He ran with the back of his fist pressed into one eye, then the other, trying to press her image away. The other hand, with the harness dangling, pushed against his heart but he could not hold the pain back. It burst free, pounding against the sharp cold air that filled his lungs.

"This is not what I wanted," he whispered as he saw the horse pass into the forest and out of sight. Hot tears burned his cheeks. "This is not what I wanted at all. None of it. None of it!"

His mind told him he was absurd to be crying. He tried to run faster to escape its judgment. His bones ached and the muscles in his legs felt as though they were tearing. He was swollen with sobs and could not contain them. His eyes flashed over the horizon looking for escape but he knew he was imprisoned by this small farm, his life caught in it, like the light caught within the raindrops. He'd have to die to fall from it, to disappear.

He wanted to run and keep running but unlike the horse, his legs hurt more with each step. Still, he was amazed that he kept going, even though the sharp air cut into his chest. There was nothing to do but run or try to. If he got to the forest he could collapse. She could not see him there. No one could see him there.

His running slowed but he couldn't stop. He coughed with the tears but he couldn't stop them either. He hated the horse. Love was crazy and he hated that he'd even bothered to feel it again. The feeling of foolishness made him sob all the more.

He ran off the path. His overalls were soon soaking and his legs were chilled. The pain numbed. He fell and rose, wet and crying like an infant, from the earth. He ran on. He no longer cared where the horse was. He saw Ian now, running into the forest, then Ian pacing his house in Baltimore in the middle of the night, every night while his wife slept, back and forth across the living room, tracing all his pain back to Miller who had failed to teach him joy, who had failed to ask what he needed, who he was. In the darkness Ian held a gun. He turned and the gun was blue in the shadows. He raised it and aimed at his father watching him, then pulled the trigger.

Pain shot through Miller's heart, crashing sharply against his ribs, then burning, then a massive explosion, bubbling up into his throat, slamming waves of nausea down into his gut, drawing the blood from his brain, arms and legs. His limbs were hollow but still tried to run. In a moment he would fall and the earth would swallow him and his life would no longer run away from him. He could catch death, if not the horse. Death would be easy to catch. He ran toward it, wanting it to crash against his sadness and shatter his body into a million raindrops. He would fall. He would fall and the black screen of endless pictures would finally darken completely.

The earth was moving now. The planet moved. The blue sky wavered, the mountain blurred. The pain increased but he could not fall and stay down. He was pulled up again and again to stumble and sweat and fall once more.

He saw the forest, the outstretched arms of evergreens silver with sunlight and rain. He could smell the pine. Finally, just as he fell for the last time and crawled against the earth, he heard the call of the horse in the distance.

There was an opening in the raindrop that hung at the tip of a quivering blade of grass above him and he crawled through into the rainbow of light inside. It was safe there, a droplet of living color. Though it was glass-like on the outside, there was no harsh reflection of his own to witness from within. There was no window. No eyes could find him here. It closed around him. He could cry forever and it would be secret. In an instant he was the light itself, a shriek of pain, a last image of his son, then he saw nothing. There was no sound and still, still, there was something.

There was something not him, yet only him. In the emptiness he knew it was the sadness that had killed him. Execution by sadness. With alarm, he sensed that whatever was here seemed amused. There was a kind of jolliness present, not ridicule, but a sense of humor that was appropriate, honest and utterly aware of the hopelessness of his life.

He knew what he was then, with or without body, eyes, wife, son, horse, land or rain. He was this, this sort of amused, detached observatory, this outpost of light.

There was a rippling within him, then the sense of floating, finally an opening. Daylight enveloped him again and a blazing mass of it collected high in the eastern sky. He blinked away his tears and realized he was looking at the sun.

He turned his head and she was there, kneeling down beside him, hands shaking as she reached out to hold him.

". . . a terrible scare," she managed to say.

"You . . ." he whispered. She removed his glasses and put them in the pocket of her apron. Miller looked up at the horse standing over them and saw his own reflection and Belle's in the watery brown eyes, two humans pressed into the earth, holding each other, sunlight all around, gulls flying over, and a mountain, blue-white and massive, in the distance.

It took them a long time to get back to the house. He leaned against her all the way. The horse walked ahead, looking back to them occasionally. When they stopped, which was often, the horse stopped, switched its tail and waited.

Several times Miller lifted his hand and opened his mouth to speak. "I've been . . . the kind of father I've been . . ." he said, and then was silent. She did not try to help him. Each time he started, she looked at him and waited. He knew this time she would wait until it came and he could make the words come. He could tell her that he didn't care about the land being sold. He could tell her about his father. In time, he could tell her everything.

She walked, looked up at him, smiled, looked away, looked back and smiled again. He began to laugh, leaning against her.

"Miller!" she said, astonished.

"Well, here we are," he said, "this awful thing has happened and I hurt. My God, how I am hurting! I can hardly move, but we're excited. We're excited, Belle."

She did not deny it. She laughed too, but nervously. It was true but she was afraid.

He liked the way she looked, her gray hair blowing all around her face, the tears stopping and starting again. He knew her childhood as he looked at her, knew the way she was long before him, loving, fearing, wanting something, crying for it, and lie after lie crushing against her, complaints about life all around her saying it wasn't glorious, voices of denial so strong that her own voice had joined them. In fact, they had both surrendered to that, Miller thought, to that. Surely *that* was not eternal.

They entered the house. The horse stood in the yard.

There was her rocker, a blue ball of yarn on the wooden table, the calendar with a Victorian Christmas scene nailed to the wall above the gleaming white stove, a yellow vase on the window sill. He saw it all with a vision that had been washed clean.

He wanted to give his eyes to her.

She put him in her chair and covered him, then rushed to the sink to rinse a cloth with warm water so she could wash his hands and face.

"I want to give you something," he said as she came to him and pressed the cloth against his skin.

There was a moment that had everything to do with time and loss, and then a moment outside of time. He seized it and with his eyes open he let himself contain the room, the day, himself and her.

"I love you," he said, and the words blew softly against her breast. Immediately he was embarrassed by all that he had been, by what he was becoming. He was boyish suddenly and foolish, but he used the embarrassment to push him to say it again. "I love you. Yes."

She looked down at him and began to tremble. She was remembering dreams that denied her, abandoned her, left her behind in the immense green darkness of the rain forest.

"I'm too old to change," she warned him.

"You're too old to change," he said back to her and smiled. "Don't change then."

He saw her greet him then, saw her clouded eyes clear and salute him, just as the horse had raised its head in salute that morning when he had entered the barn. He knew love when it spoke to him, the terrible grace of love, demanding and forgiving. No answers. No promises.

He greeted her in return.

*ANDREA CARLISLE*
*Vol. 7#3, 1983*

Evenings, Gran sat on the side porch of the farmhouse, reading and watching the sky. She liked doing two things at once and had rigged an extra-long cord on the floorlamp so she could take it out of the bedroom onto the porch with her. She'd switch it on as soon as it began to get dark. The lamp had a huge red shade, cracked and curled in places, blotched with dew from the evenings when she'd forgotten to take it back in the house. From where I swung on the gate by the road, it lit her face in a strange way—half her chin, one side of her nose, and her eyelashes; half a face lit up against the tall, dark corn that grew right up to the house.

She'd look up from her book and lean out of the lamp's glow to check on the stars coming out. The electric light would travel over her head as she leaned, through her wispy grey hair with its little curls at her nape, across her wide shoulders and down her back. As she leaned, I'd study the patch of sweater illuminated at the small of her back—its black and silver strands running off into the dark.

Sometimes I got curious about what she was reading. Then I'd sneak into the house through the front door, tiptoe up to the windows in the bedroom and look over her shoulder. She read Shakespeare and *Prevention* magazine, books of philosophy and religion, though she was definitely not religious; an atheist in fact. The only time I read over her shoulder for long was when she was reading a mystery story, which wasn't very often.

That particular night in October, I remember, she looked out at the sky more than she read. In fact, when it got dark, she never even turned on the lamp. Though a book lay open on her lap, she studied the sky the whole time, while the sun set purple. Out of the dark she called suddenly, distinctly. By the time I climbed down from the gate and reached the porch, she'd vanished inside, taking the lamp with her.

When Grandfather died, she'd decided to stay put right there in Wisconsin, so she rented out the land. But because the renter had insisted on the full acre, she had to get used to the wall of corn where her backyard had been. There'd been other changes, such as the windows. She'd torn out the wall between the bedroom and the porch and, in its place, bolted together a bunch of storm windows to make a crude glass wall facing the hayfield, so she could see outdoors from her bed. Her habits had become even more pronounced, especially her porch time. We chattered and argued through most of the days of the weekends my parents let me visit her; but when the sun began to sink and she picked up her book, I knew I had to leave her alone. There'd be no dinner, either, till the sun had set and the stars were shining. Then, stirring mushroom sauce into rice, or sneaking a little of her vegetarian goulash into my hamburger, she'd begin to talk to me again, as abruptly as she'd left off.

The local people knew of this habit—that she sat out on the porch of an evening with a book. Luvern, driving by in the creamery truck, would call out hello to her on the porch. She wouldn't answer. If I was there, he'd stop a minute. He'd wish me a good evening and in an especially loud voice, would remind me to call on him across the valley, if any of us two women needed a hand. She wouldn't answer and I was proud of that. She was like a queen in her silence. So that strange night I hurried in, curious to know why she'd left the porch so abruptly.

She was standing at the stove, cutting red onions into the beans. When I asked her why she'd called me, she looked surprised and shrugged. I put my arms around her and felt her relax. Then she laughed, shoved me away with her butt and opened the refrigerator.

"I don't know why, but I was going to tell you to come in out of the dark. Go back on out if you like, stay out all goddam night. You're twelve, it's your life."

"If you don't mind Gran, I'll eat dinner. It's nine o'clock."

We ate the main course and then argued over whole wheat or white flour to go into the brownies. We both liked to make a dessert and then eat it right away. By the time we climbed into bed, it would always be late. The jazz show would come on the public radio station, the only station Gran allowed, and she'd insist that we sing along as we brushed our hair, humming and la-la-laing over the unfamiliar music. Sometimes we'd eat apples, too, singing with our mouths full, then putting the cores in a bowl by the bedside table. Gran called it vice. She brushed her hair in short jerks, while I languorously undid my pigtail and stroked and stroked my wavy hair. It was the only time I can remember being allowed to brush as long as I liked. I watched us in the windows, brushing and brushing, and the outline of the woodpile like a faint double exposure beyond us, and the lush alfalfa, edged by the cornfield, and finally the woods. Above the woods was a thin stripe of starry sky cut off by the peaked roof. When Gran turned the light out, the night would invade the room. The glass wall made me feel half out of doors. I pulled the sheet immediately over my head, and we'd snuggle down under the covers, five layers of blankets in October for when the fire went dead later on in the night.

Later that night, I stirred in my sleep. I felt Gran curled beside me, smelling of onions and talc. It gradually dawned on me that her breathing was quiet and much too regular. She was awake. I opened my eyes and noticed, then, the strange shadow on the wall. Then I saw the man standing by the bed. He had a thick stick of stove wood in his hands and was raising it slowly over his head. I drew in my breath to scream and Gran reached over and put her hand on my arm.

"I'm glad you found the firewood," she said clearly. "We left the door open for you, and now, if you'll build up the fire, I'll cook your dinner. There's a place for you to sleep here." She sat up in bed.

He lowered the stick of wood and stood for a minute. "But I'm dirty," he mumbled.

"Would you like to wash?"

"No, ma'am."

"You don't have to then. Susan, will you fill the kettle please. And we'll need more firewood, so if you'd bring in eight or nine more sticks."

The man walked out the porch door toward the woodpile. We hadn't even seen his face yet.

"Gran," I whispered, "do you know him?"

"Put the kettle on," she said.

She turned the light on in the kitchen, the little light under its copper shade that lit the table just enough for a midnight snack. She relit the burner under the leftover beans. The man came back into the house with his arms full of wood. I heard his boots clunk heavily across the floor, though I hadn't dared look at him yet. I filled the kettle and reached down the jars of instant coffee and Creamora. Over my shoulder I heard the rustle of newspaper and a match striking against the top of the cast iron heat stove.

Gran appeared beside me at the cookstove, rummaging around the pan shelf for the leftover brownies.

"Why don't you sit down," she said to the man.

"Maybe," he said. And in a minute he drew a chair out from the table and sat down.

"You remind me something of my grandson, Johnny. Susan here, her brother. I never get to see enough of him. Are you from someplace around here?"

I had no brother named Johnny, no brother at all. I turned to look at the man, then. His dark hair was messed and his ears stuck out oddly through his hair. He looked nothing like me. He was hot now that the fire was going, and I watched him take off his hunting jacket, noticing that when he lifted his hands from the table, he'd left smudges on the cloth. His hands were dark and greasy. I saw a stripe of red across his palm under the light.

"You've cut yourself," Gran said, and she put a bowl of bean soup in front of him, with the pan of brownies. I watched incredulously as she sat down with him at the table. She leaned her chin on her elbows and when he reached for a brownie, their arms nearly touched.

"I hope you like that kind of whole flour they mill in town, because Susan and I had an argument. She favors the white stuff from Milwaukee, but I over-ruled her."

He took a brownie and dipped it into his soup, pushing a piece of celery into the spoon and then cramming the brownie into his mouth after the spoonful of soup. I watched his face to see if he'd realize what he'd done—the sweet brownie with the salty, oniony soup. He looked nervously at Gran. I heard my own voice, thin, reedy.

"I don't know," I began.

"Susan," Gran said, "give the man his coffee."

"Gran, you know what Mother would say."

"Oh, young lady, chatter, chatter. I think it's time to get you back to bed."

"Your sink is dripping," he said suddenly.

"Yeah, I told Johnny a dozen times, but he doesn't seem to find the time. Maybe he doesn't know how."

"A wrench," he said.

"Let me see what I can find." Gran crossed the kitchen and opened the cupboard under the sink. "You handy at this sort of thing?"

He shrugged, pushed the bowl away from him, half full, and opened and closed his hands. Gran found a box of rubber washers and pulled them out. He poured them out into the sink. Gran found Grandfather's big wrench. It took her two hands to lift it. For a second I thought she'd hit him with it. I hoped and prayed she'd hit him. But she only set the wrench on the sideboard.

Gesturing at the sink, she said, "I think it just naturally drips. I'll make the bed up for you. Go on, Susan, I'll tuck you in, in a minute."

"Tuck me in!" I said. She raised her eyebrows. I looked longingly at the wall phone over the table.

"Can I call Mom?" I said.

"No, honey, it's the middle of the night."

"But, Gran," I said.

"Susan," she said sharply, "go right to bed now and no more annoying us." I searched her face for some sort of signal. She must've been afraid, but I saw nothing but annoyance, more annoyance than I'd ever seen before in my grandmother.

"All right!" I said, annoyed myself, and I stomped out of the room.

"Teenagers these days," she said to him.

"That girl a teenager?"

"Oh, she's twelve, she's a teenager," Gran said. I pulled the covers tight around me and turned on the red lamp overhead. I heard Gran moving farther away in the house; then the sound of metal on metal as he put the wrench on the faucet. The dripping got faster, then stopped. I heard Gran call out across the house, "You tired?"

"Tired," he said. "I'll tell the world."

I heard their footsteps moving away. Gran said, "Good night, now, Johnny," and she came back into the bedroom. She turned the switch off over my head, and picked up a book and the lamp and stepped towards the door.

"Gran," I hissed from bed. "I want you."

"Susan, you just mind yourself. This is my porch time and I want to see the sun rise in peace." And she put on socks and pulled her sweater over her nightgown, and then curled up in her reading chair beyond the windows and switched on the lamp. I lay in the dark, watching her from the window, her hair tousled into little cowlicks, lit red by the lamp, and the soft skin of her cheek, powdered red. She looked smaller, somehow, sitting in the middle of the Wisconsin night with her lamp. I crept to the glass and looked over her shoulder. She was reading the Bible! Gran, who hardly believed in God, was reading the Old Testament:

"Mark the doorposts," I read with her, "And none of you shall go out of the house until morning. For the Lord will pass over the door. And when your children say, what do you mean by this, you shall say that the Lord passed over the houses of the people of Israel in Egypt and did them no harm. But Pharaoh rose up in the night, with his firstborn dead in his arms, and called Moses and Aaron to take their people out of slavery and be gone."

I tapped the window. Gran turned the page. I got back into bed. If she could stay up, so could I. I gripped the bedpost to keep awake, but the house was uncommonly warm from the firewood and I slid down the pillow. I woke up to see the man stepping out the door onto the porch. I saw Gran turn to him. The sky behind them was a glory of light purple; the stars, gorgeous, prickly; and a stripe of orange was widening above the woods. She put her finger to her lips. He gave a nod, then crashed off through the corn. I drifted off again.

But the morning came on brightly. There was a knock at the door and I got up to answer it, seeing Gran slumped snoring into her book. The sheriff stood there and Luvern was with him. I brought them in and made them coffee, roused Gran and she came in, smoothing her hair with her hand.

The sheriff cleared his throat a couple times, but it was Luvern who finally spoke. "I guess I should tell you, Rose Ellen . . . " he stopped a minute, then began speaking again. "It's just that I'm surprised to be talking to you. Somebody . . . killed a lot of the neighbors last night. You've got empty houses on three sides."

Then Gran phoned my mother. She asked her to come out and get me right away. She hung up the phone and sat down. Her face wobbled. She sobbed and shook a long time, while Luvern knelt beside her and the sheriff leaned against the sink, cracking his knuckles.

I thought Gran would move away, but she didn't. She told them all she felt safer at her place than she would in a cement fortress. As time went on, the empty farms around her were bought up by people from out of the county, people who weren't so susceptible to the story. I was never allowed to stay over alone at Gran's again, though it wasn't because she told my parents about our visitor. I was the one who couldn't stop talking about him, even when my parents said it made them nervous.

Sometimes, at least, there'd be family reunions out at Gran's place. When her porch time came around, the family would joke among themselves about how she was alone in all this quiet most of the time anyway. As for me, I'd go quietly to stand at the glass and read over her shoulder as the night fell. I don't think Gran slept straight through the night much anymore. In the morning when we awoke, more often than not she'd be out in her reading chair again, asleep under the glow of the red lamp.

*MARISHA CHAMBERLAIN*
*Vol. 5#1, 1980*

*Shelly and Her Sister Mim*        *black and white photograph*        *ANNE NOGGLE*
*Vol. 9#2&3, 1986*

*Mother and Daughter*
*San Pedro del Norte,*
*Nicaragua/Honduras border*

*black and white photograph*
*Vol. 7#3, 1983*

MARGARET RANDALL

*Acoma Woman*      *black and white photograph*      MARGARET RANDALL
                   *Vol. 9#2&3, 1986*

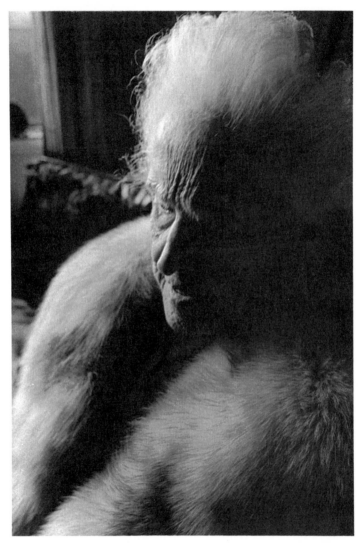

*Agnes in Fur Collar*　　　　　　　　　　　　*ANNE NOGGLE*
*black and white photograph*
*Vol. 9#2&3, 1986*

*Always Looking*  DEBORAH KLIBANOFF
*black and white photograph*
*Vol. 9#2&3, 1986*

*The Dance*                    *woodcut*                    MYRNA A. YODER
                              *15" x 15½"*
                              *Vol. 10#1, 1986*
                              *photo by David Reinert*

*Seeds*      *prismacolor pencil on paper*        RENÉE ROMANOWSKI
                    *18" x 24"*
               *Vol. 7#1, 1982*

*Stroke*    *color pencil and crayon on paper*    ELIZABETH LAYTON
                        *22" x 28"*
                    *Vol. 9#2&3, 1986*

Self-Portrait          *intaglio*          MARTHA WEHRLE
                    4½" x 6"
                  *Vol. 1#2, 1976*

*Maria in Memory*　　　*fabric and thread*　　　*DEIDRE SCHERER*
*19" x 23½"*
*Vol. 9#2&3, 1986*

*W*e cull these variegated and pungent blossoms for our bouquet and place it as a centerpiece within women's space, in a safe-house. We offer it as a vision to provide guidance, inspiration, and hope along the path of our difficult journey.

Virginia Woolf observed that "women have served . . . as looking glasses possessing the magic and delicious power of reflecting the figure of man at twice its natural size." Now we are learning to be mirrors for each other, reflecting not distortions but true images. The following essays by *Calyx* contributors are a response to the editors' solicitation concerning the influences on their work during *Calyx*'s first decade. While the essays are varied in approach, a commonality surfaces in the way the authors have been affected by the work of other women. We hear the continuation of the dialogue between women in these voices as they resonate with the importance of discovering our *her*story and with the empowerment found in the recognition of the women in the mirrors as ourselves.

After the divorce, I had new territory, much like the Oklahoma land run when a piece of land was claimed & had to be settled. I had spent years hiding behind my husband, the children & housework. Now the land & sky were open. That's what's frightening about the prairie at first—its barrenness & lack of shelter. I had always written, and now my sense of place was defined by whatever mattered at the time. I picked up my Indian heritage & began a journey toward *ani-yun-wiyu,* the Cherokee word for "real people."

I read journals, magazines, poetry, some fiction. I saw that feelings could be expressed in writing—feelings of bewilderment & fear, especially anger. It was a trend in women's writing—the pulley I needed out of the separation & isolation I felt without the surroundings of family. I saw women come to grips with themselves. The vulnerability, the struggle, the agonizing choices. I had to find a homestead within myself, or invent one. I dug a potato cellar.

Family had covered the fissures in my life. Now I had fragments/shards/whatever the territory offered. My poems & writing were the land I cultivated. I moved toward "being" in poetry. A struggle for survival. My purpose was to find the truth of what I was, my voice, what I had to offer. I could not have done it without the other voices— the sun & rain & soil for myself as a person. The pleasure of being a woman.

I found that I weathered the prairie storms and the limitations that came with the territory. I found acceptance of myself, the strength to travel prairie roads & talk about poetry in towns where farmers in the cafes stare. I relived the struggle to claim the land, establish a sod house, plow the fields, milk the cow. The rest will come. All this is an internal land, of course. I started late with only a map given to me by other women who said the territory was there. It was a fertile landscape just inside the head. I had only to load the wagon, hitch the horses. A journey that my mother never made before she folded up her camp.

I learned to trust images. I could even experiment with words. Put muffler, glass packs on the wagon—mud flaps if I wanted. I have what men have had—liberty to be myself. Maybe women had it too & I just never knew. Wrong/right/whatever. Now I could throw out the ice cubes/find my severed limbs/sew them on instead of giving heart & arms & lungs away. I have use for them on the edge of the frontier, saw-edge after saw-edge.

The glory of the plain self in search of words to say "the self"/the delight of it. The birth, the shedding of invisibility. The pursuit of "she-pleasure." SHEDONISM.

The themes/form/experimental forms. Words as house & shed & outbuildings on the land. The urgency. The cessation of pounding myself/hanging my separate parts to dry on low branches & rocks. It's women who influenced my work. Their courage, their trend toward revelation. I am on the journey to the *ani-yun-wiyu.*

*DIANE GLANCY*

Some words, some lines, some books get snagged in my head and linger. Last month it was the word *rearranged* brought to life in Mary Oliver's new book, *Dream Work*. For days I saw the black bear moving sluggishly as the earth warmed.

> *In the distance*
> *the ice began to boom and wrinkle*
> *and a dampness*
> *that could not be defeated began*
> *to come from her, her breathing*
> *enlarged, oh, tender mountain, she rearranged*
> *herself so that the cubs*
> *could slide from her body, so that the rivers*
> *would flow.*

(from *Driving Through the Wind River Reservation: A Poem of Black Bear*)

I felt myself inside that bear's dark, thick fur, felt my body *rearranging*. What skill to heed the flickers and shimmers of our world with such care, to record nature with such reverence. What skill to set that word so carefully on the line. Mary Oliver, whom I may never meet, was teaching me the craft of poetry. Such teachers are many. And for me, such teachers are usually female, teachers attentive to our entanglements.

Most are poets, though I remember the freedom I felt when I saw Ntozake Shange's *for colored girls who have considered suicide/when the rainbow is enuf*, a work inviting me to dare such abandon. I remember wistfully when my days allowed time with the works of Toni Morrison, Mary Gordon, Maxine Hong Kingston, all describing women who emerged. I remember a recent PBS special on Georgia O'Keeffe, stark as the Southwest landscape she loved. I still smile at her laughing confession that by painting huge flowers, she *forced* us to notice, a comment I've related to the work of minority writers.

We too seek to force a society to notice the bitter and the sweet. Usually we are both community participants and solitary writers, a tension. The mere cover of Denise Levertov's *The Poet in the World* reminds me of her firm conviction: "Both life and poetry fade, wilt, shrink when they are divorced." No need to choose as some would urge. Alice Walker, Toni Cade Bambara, Lorna Dee Cervantes are thick in the struggle of their people, and their writing is part of that struggle. Though the daily realities—high drop-out rate, low per capita income, high unemployment—continue, these women teach me that the arrangement and rearrangement of work on the page is neither elitist nor irrelevant. It is the appropriate task of the person who weaves words for her people's use. Though I seldom see them, *mis colegas Chicanas* diminish my loneliness. Sandra, Ana, Beverly, Denise, Teresa, Vangie, Helena, Rosemary struggle with me to bear witness to a culture sensual as ripe mango. How often I have reread Annie Dillard's statement, "The thing is to stalk your calling in a certain skilled and supple way, to locate the most tender and live spot and plug into that pulse." For me and for many minority writers, that pulse is both our gender and our ethnicity.

It's the poets to whom I return over and over. Their writing gives me hope. The "common language" is real. Adrienne Rich wrote, "in order to write I have to believe that there is someone willing to collaborate subjectively." I am. And women writers steadily feed me as Rukeyser said they would. Not that the fare is all warm comfort. I reread Linda Pastan. Her poems such as "Routine Mammogram" say truths we know sadly—temporal, these bodies. I hear Levertov's outrage at our complacency toward human suffering, hear her urging us "Not to forget but to remember better." A Sharon Olds poem can make me gasp, shut the book as the poem moves through me, poems of deep, dark motherlove:

> That look of attention
> on the face of the young mother
> like an animal
> bending over the carriage, looking up
> ears erect, eyes showing
> the whites all around.

(from *Young Mothers I*)

Olds states the private—thoughts, words, images—too raw to arrange and **rearrange**. But she does. Startling.

As Atwood startled me around 1980. Her *I approach this love / like a biologist / pulling on my rubber / gloves & white lab coat* drew me back again and again to the dusty poetry section of the library, the spell only broken when I sat down one day with lined **paper** and a number-two pencil.

But new spells are cast. Now I dream of journeying to watch the weavers in Chiapas, to see their hands link generations, to watch as they confront their "white space," create their poetic designs. I long to get tangled and snagged in their threads, then break that spell my paper/pencil way, sitting alone as my unseen teachers do, re-arranging words on the page.

This week's *New York Times Book Review* has an excerpt from Adrienne Rich's remarks when she received the National Book Award in 1974. When she accepted it on behalf of the three women nominated—Audre Lorde, Adrienne Rich, Alice Walker—she stated, "We believe that we can enrich ourselves more in supporting and giving to each other than by competing against each other . . . ." The poets, writers, artists who most deeply affect my work teach me not only about craft but also about values, harmony. The first time I met Denise Levertov, a poet whose humanity I had long admired, she did what I hope we can all do for one another as women. "My dear," she said, "if you're going to give a reading, you'll need water." She returned a few minutes later bearing a paper cup as I stood there mouth open. My unseen mentors teach me not only about rearranging words: they teach me about rearranging a life.

*PAT MORA*

SPLITTING OPEN: FINDING SHARON OLDS'S
"YOUNG MOTHERS IX"                                    *INGRID WENDT*

Three days after the birth of my daughter, this dream. I am holding my daughter, this squalling marvel I love with a thunder I never—during all those natural childbirth classes, those practiced deep breathings, those hours painting the second-hand crib—never could have for one moment imagined. In my dream I am lifting her out of the kitchen sink bath water, trying to balance her head in my hand, her body along the length of my arm in the football hold the visiting nurse taught me (after I'd called her, in tears, "I've never given a baby a bath!"). Lifting her out of the sink that isn't a sink but a nursery basket, one of many in rows stacked four or five high, like cages chickens are kept in. Lifting a chicken out of its cage and placing it carefully onto the chopping block, meat cleaver whacking off legs. Thighs. Wings. Faster now, splitting the breast. Chicken? No: Daughter! Unable to scream, I wake up, fearing my sanity, fearing this love for this baby so strong it turns into murder, so strong I cannot look again at this dream, this guilt, this fierce aberration of motherlove I never would (until now) tell anyone. Certainly never thought to put in a poem. Where was the context? (Hormones, probably.) Who had ever felt this before? (No one.) Where was the language of ecstasy, wildness, ferocity rolled into one? (It didn't exist.)

And so I continued to love my daughter, to fear for her safety while learning to care for her, soon quite adroit with kitchen sink bath, never dreaming anything like that again, almost forgetting the dream. Almost forgetting that something inside me, again deeply hidden, wasn't quite right, although I knew what it was, was real, was true.

What I did write, instead, was equally true, though opposite. Happy, writing of happiness, of holding my daughter, nursing her in that incredible silence where nothing else exists—where past and present and future are mystically one—I tried to capture the awe, the sense of discovery, the blurs of identity I hadn't expected to feel. I was not I, but my mother, my daughter. Paradox set within paradox. Package of hand-painted Russian nesting dolls.

What a wonder to find, six years later, Sharon Olds's poem "Young Mothers IX" in *Calyx* (Vol. 2#2), with these lines:

> *The baby is beautiful as an angel and the young mother*
> *dreams of animals tied up and burned alive.*
>
> *Between the language of sentiment*
> *and the language of hell*
> *she cannot speak.*

And further on:

> *It is true that the young woman, a mother for*
> *three days, would die for her child*
> *and dreams every night of murder.*
>
> . . .
>
> *There is no language here, no word that means*
> *hell and the mother and sex.*

What a relief!

Someone else (incredibly) had gone through something like my own experience (and if one woman, maybe more). I was validated (there really had not, until this poem, been a language for this experience; Sharon Olds said as much). What relief, and pleasure, too, in finding that in the space of one page a poet had given to this experience what poets have for centuries given: a name. And, for me, this revelation: here was a poet who'd dared what I never had thought to dare.

"What would happen if one woman told the truth about her life?" Muriel Rukeyser once wrote, and answered, "The world would split open." Of course, I'd believed her. I'd quoted these words to students and often, to myself. But had I taken the words to heart? Apparently not. At least, not enough.

Maybe what I'm trying to say has something to do with learning about trust and courage. Trust in experience. Courage to put it in words, no matter how strange or seeming to lack a context. Maybe I learned, too, the inescapable implications of Virginia Woolf's saying that we think, we write, through our mothers. And if sometimes there are none? Then we mother ourselves, and our daughters, and our sisters. We create, for ourselves and for them, a new language: a context for what we know to be true.

Not to say that I always, since finding this poem, succeed. Nor am I sure how much my own writing has changed. What I am sure of, however, is that my resolve has been strengthened. My inner eye has opened still wider. And I am grateful to Sharon Olds for having written this poem.

*INGRID WENDT*

*Once upon a time a woman was given a multicolored ball of silken yarn. Each thread in the ball appeared to be inextricably entangled within all the others. Her task was to follow each thread to its brilliant source and if she was able to do this a great truth would be revealed to her.*

*She began by choosing a brilliant red thread, and as she worked her way through its tangled path she found, unexpectedly, that the single red strand had become orange, and that the orange became yellow, and then green and blue, and indigo and then violet, and when she reached the end of the violet thread, surrounding her was the entire ball of yarn in one unimaginably long single strand. She learned that what had appeared to be many was one, and what was one was made of the many.*

Determining the influence on my work by other women artists creates a tangled mass of ideas, each interwoven in the structure of the others.

I realize that I am unable to distinguish whether those writings, those paintings, that music have directly shifted and expanded my own perceptions or if I am drawn to these works because my impulses and obsessions have *already* begun to move me in this direction. The works of certain women function as "markers" along my path that reinforce and strengthen my own beliefs because I know that they are shared by others. I realize that each of these possibilities is enfolded within the other, each influencing the other and, in truth, each creating the other.

So it is appropriate to begin with gratitude to Eleanor Wilner, poet and friend, whose work frequently functions as a counterbalance to my own. Her poetry brings me a clarity of mind, an opposite perception, a vision of the world not previously considered in *my* ordering of the universe. Both of us, inevitably, sift from each other's work the nuggets of our own obsessions. *We alter what we see,* she says in the lovely poem, "two pairs of eyes."

Most of the other women I think of as affecting me/my work either have validated my way of seeing myself in relation to the world, or have illuminated whatever may be my current obsession in a way I hadn't thought about before.

In the 1970s, as I needed to understand and re-claim the as yet unacknowledged female power inside myself, the feminist journal *Heresies* published a "Great Goddess" issue with strong female imagery in works by Anne Healy, Louise Bourgeois, and Mary Beth Edelson. These works became a model for me of powerful, spiritual art by women.

I remember at that time reading an article by Lucy Lippard in which she wrote about where and how women create art—on kitchen tables, in bedrooms, basements, in patchwork bits of here-and-there time. And still the work is powerful! I have always preferred having a studio in my house. However, the only model of a "real" artist I had at that time was of someone (male) having a loft (preferably in New York) and being dedicated to art twenty-four hours a day (at least). Lippard's article gave me permission to take myself and my work seriously, AS I AM, in all my multifaceted roles, each enhancing and enlivening the others.

As my obsessions shifted from Goddess imagery, through right/left brain thinking, to the idea of multidimensional realities mutually co-existing, a line from Cynthia Ozik's book *The Cannibal Galaxy* remained a powerful one for me: "What we deem to be Reality is only Partial Possibility coarsely ground into mere dumb Matter, a physicist's model framed on the crude armature of gravity and chemicals." It became one of the "markers" along my path, stating in precise and elegant language what I had been expressing in my own work.

There are women artists whom I have never met working in the city in which I live who sustain me and enliven me with their energy. Some, like Karen Guzak and Isabel Sim-Hamilton, affect me because I believe we all are working on the same obsession: that there are a multiplicity of realities mutually co-existing, that these other realities whether within ourselves or outside this universe are our shadows—always with us, rarely acknowledged.

There are other women in my city whose work is so different from mine (Fay Jones, Gloria De Arcangelis, Sherry Markovitz), and whose outrageous exuberance and humor fuel my own creativity precisely because it is so opposite from what I do.

Each of these women, and in truth many others, nourish and sustain my growth as an artist. Each enhances me as a human being intent on fulfilling my part in this vast dance of the Universe. And each, in her own way, helps me to feel a part of ALL THAT IS.

*FAEDRA KOSH*

Ten years ago I had been out of college for a year, gotten married, and was working in a photographic department in a drug store. Although I had finished a degree in Fine Arts, I did not pursue any creative projects for about two years. It wasn't until my mother died that I started to think seriously about painting again; maybe a reaction to revelations of mortality. I set up a table in my living room and did a watercolor of a house plant. That led to more plants, which progressed to flowers and then to sensuous close-ups of roses. These plant images started to become very symmetrical and very centered. These images were quite different from the work I had done in school, although one of my women instructors did take us to the university greenhouses to sketch, and those were some of my favorite assignments.

Then one day a friend of mine gave me a copy of Judy Chicago's book *Through The Flower.* As I read it I discovered that my own isolated development was very similar to hers and those of other women artists. There it was, in print; what I had been experiencing for a year, alone in my living room, unaware of any kind of "female imagery" occurring in the art world. It was an eye-opening concept that because I was a woman I might create imagery arising partly out of my own physicality. It was an amazing revelation to me and I felt part of a greater whole. This awakening helped me get through a difficult time. It was a transitory time between school and creating a language of my own. I identified with Judy Chicago at this time, but as my work progressed I identified less with specific artists and more with events in my life and the world.

Part of my development resulted from stubbornly defying trends in art that I considered insincere. I didn't consider neo-expressionism anything new, and the "bad" art that was being done just seemed to be saying, "Look how bad this is." "Bad" can only be taken so far before it gets stale. So I went down my own path, a path with the proverbial "forks in the road." You choose one fork and leave the other, never knowing the fate you may have missed. It seems once the artist chooses one of the forks, she can never get back to the original point of departure; the time and frame of mind have changed.

The next phase of my development manifested itself in small, tedious, repetitive shapes. Furniture, clothing and home interiors started showing up; household objects, personal themes; down a linear evolutionary path, like reliving one's life in a cathartic process. One of my father's favorite Latin phrases was "ontogeny recapitulates phylogeny." It describes the biological process of human gestation in which the fetus reproduces in its own evolution all the progressing stages of animal development. It seems my work went through a developmental evolution.

Even though I had been educated in art, these first pieces were fairly naive and unaffected, but unfortunately I started to notice the art world and other artists. Being exposed to other artists' work isn't bad. I've been inspired by Frida Kahlo, Miriam

Shapiro, Helen Frankenthaler, Louise Bourgeois, Georgia O'Keeffe and, in my student days, my instructors, Linda Okasaki and Jo Hockenhull. But the influences of the *system* that's been created in the art world can be detrimental. You start to enter competitions, send out slides to galleries and get your resumé assembled. In essence, you compete, and that is a negative influence. In that respect, exposure to the art system can be harmful to the pursuit of honest work. So you've got to somehow ignore the "careerism" and "hype" and do strong, personal work at the same time you're out there trying to get your art shown.

That takes me back to the woman artist who has had the greatest influence on my art, philosophically if not stylistically: Georgia O'Keeffe. Her work is a powerful, individual statement and her career has weathered many fads and fashions. It's hard to label her style, though many art critics have tried. Her vision prevailed. O'Keeffe was not a feminist. She denied any presence of "female imagery" in her work. She did not work for women's causes or for the advancement of other women artists, but the sheer strength and will of O'Keeffe continuing to paint was enough to inspire and influence any artist, woman or man, to "go home and work" as she once advised. Even as she began to go blind she continued to work, and in the later years of her career created sculptures when she could no longer see. Even if it were possible to copy her style, it would be negating the very lesson her life taught: paint the way your personality dictates even though it may not be currently in style. Trends are ephemeral and if the trend isn't sincere it will soon be passé anyway. The power of O'Keeffe's vision permeates all of her work. Somehow it's those influences that have to sustain the artist through the daily grind of frustration and rejection that wear away at idealism and spirit. Her example of strength and independence is what makes a lasting impression on me.

O'Keeffe rejected the idea of being labeled a woman artist, or doing "female imagery"; maybe she disliked being labeled, or being segregated from her male counterparts, and maybe she had the right idea. The women's movement has done a lot to make up for the decades of society's ignorance of women artists, but the ultimate goal is not to be a separate group but to be integrated with all artists. I hope we can come to a time when we can all participate in a system free of politics and labels.

*JENNIFER STABLER-HOLLAND*

*BARBARA THOMAS*

It seems that no matter what our background or circumstance of birth, to be born American means that we will believe in miracles. It means that we will relate to things as they should be and not as they are. It means that we are programmed to need more than we can ever use, and to live waiting for that once-in-a-lifetime opportunity that will set us apart from all others. We are stars, each one of us. We struggle between the real and the ideal to place ourselves in the best position to catch the light that shines here in the land of boundless growth, endless promise and eternal youth.

As painting students, we learned form and technique, and to watch those just ahead of us, who were rumored to occupy a space where they hover just above earth, on the cutting edge. They were described in many ways: abstract expressionist, minimalist, conceptualist, and all were avant-garde. They were the model for success; the bad boy young rebels preparing the future. Running along at their side were the critics who would shout back to the rest of us about what it was really like out there, and what it was we could expect when we finally arrived.

As students we were encouraged to question technique and material, but rarely content and purpose. Content was manifest in the art's being, so to question was a bothersome detail. As practicing young rebels preparing to exist on the periphery of society, we were responsible to nothing and no one but the artwork itself. That was our purpose, our *raison d'être*. As for the rest of the world, it was their problem to catch up with us.

. . .

Now I am a graduate, practicing good art, and good art is responsible only to itself. I and my former classmates are in the marketplace, and we are there to sell. Many are already in good galleries, winning awards and showing in museums. My former class-mates tell me we must document everything. They say if you are not selling it's only because you are failing in the new religion: marketing. They say you can sell anything if you can find your audience. To market yourself well is to communicate with your public. I ask seriously, "Is communication a part of the work or a part of the selling?" I ask again, as I had years earlier, "What is our purpose, to whom or what are we respon-sible?"

All this vision and nothing to do but please myself and art. It's an approach in which some have found happiness, fame and prosperity. I, instead, find myself falling, while straining to see more. Over and over I tumble, until I roll out of the postgraduate sunlight and find myself on the forest floor. It is cool and moist here at the base of the trees, where mushrooms grow, and there is the sweet musty smell of decaying leaves. It is here in the shade that I first encounter the dark haunting images of Diane Arbus. She draws my attention with a whisper of super-real harshness. In her portraits, I see faces of men and women, some bag ladies, street people, and prostitutes. I see a place in her work where life and death can occupy the same space. It is not always an attractive view, but it is acceptable because it offers a possibility of growing old, to which most else around me would not admit. In the face of an eight-year-old, she reveals a potential murderer, and I turn inward to face the murderer in myself and the possibility of holding it there as a balance to the pure light of my ideals. I am attracted to her lush shadows, which are wrapped in the reality of our fears, our crippled misshapen selves, and our nightmares of imperfection. I discover in Arbus's work the power of the mundane, of the plain, unimpressive moments. She offers something, as Lewis Hyde explains in his book *The Gift*, that comes to us on the gift economy, and no matter the market price it can only be given, not sold.

Alice Walker speaks to me with the tale of power and responsibility she weaves in *The Color Purple*. She tells of a powerful character who, in his fear, uses power irresponsibly. In this character she shows us the burdens that inevitably go along with power, that power is relative, and that no one is free of its consequences, even if one chooses to ignore its results. She shows us how a victim can unknowingly carry the seeds of her own salvation, and that it is a mistake to think that liberation can only be given. She shows us that victim and oppressor are not so different, and that no man or woman holds grace and salvation in their exclusive domain. I realize that to accept power without responsibility is folly. I can choose to be responsible for the consequences of my ideas, and for my conduct on this planet.

I do not conclude that all art must tell a story or teach a lesson. To relegate people or art to any one purpose seems foolish. I am drawn to artists like Arbus and Walker whose work is honest in content and execution and is relevant across time and cultures.

BARBARA THOMAS

Memories and emotions erupted as I reread an article that had been buried in a scrapbook for 18 years. Set in large black type on the front page of the Ashland, Oregon, February 14, 1968, edition of the *Daily Tidings* were the headlines "Ashland Artist Stirs a Ruckus," with the subtitle "Three Nudes." I was the guilty artist and my disturbing painting, "No Exit," had been on display in Salem, Oregon, at the Capitol coffee shop along with the works of other Southern Oregon artists.

Inspired by Jean Paul Sartre's existentialist view of humanity and his play, "No Exit," I created a symbolic interpretation of this theme. I painted two women and a man, nude and trapped together in a room, but incapable of fulfilling each other's need for love or compassion. Ironically, when freedom was granted, the challenge and insecurity of the unknown became even more threatening, and all three chose to remain trapped together with "No Exit."

A Capitol coffee shop waitress who considered my imagery offensive and "in poor taste" had my painting moved to the janitor's closet. As a result of this censorship, "No Exit" became a curiosity which people lined up to view. The ruckus caused by this unconventional painting was subsequently discussed by a UPI reporter in the press, and I was interviewed on television. I told the reporter, "I want my paintings to raise questions, not merely to decorate," but "Oregon isn't ready for nudes."

As a newcomer to Oregon, I decided to remain undaunted by unacceptance. I had grown up in New York City but earned my academic degrees in Los Angeles, arriving in Oregon in 1964 to join the faculty of Southern Oregon State College. During my early years in Ashland, I was shocked by certain images as well as the lack of them; the college faculty women identified themselves as a social group under the name "Purple Girdles," and life drawing was not included in the Art Department's curriculum until 1968. As the college expanded, I remained the only full-time woman faculty member in the art department until 1982.

Anxious to do more than survive, and to grow and contribute on a different level than my predecessor, I gradually realized I would have to reach beyond Ashland. However, when I did, I was not always in tune with what I saw. For example, the early collaborative efforts of Miriam Shapiro and Judy Chicago from the Fresno Women's Center, with their use of the circle or vagina image to symbolize woman's essence, seemed as limited and repressive to me as the title, "Purple Girdles."

The turning point in my perspective on women and art was 1976 when I attended my first College Art Association meeting and a meeting of the Women's Caucus for Art. I realized then that the women's art movement was growing from a broad foundation of historical scholarship and artistic diversity.

Attending the panel "How to Teach the Course, Women and Art" dramatically enhanced my teaching ability; for the first time I heard women artists and scholars contribute their diverse views, as well as offer the necessary tools, books, films, slides, and encouragement to initiate this vital course. The panelists included Judy Loeb, author of *Feminist Collage;* Elsa Honig Fine, author of *Women Artists,* and later founder and editor of the *Woman's Art Journal;* and Karen Peterson and J. J. Wilson, who wrote *Women and Art.*

In reviewing my personal development as an artist, I realized my work has evolved through several thematic and stylistic phases. In the 1960s I felt isolated from the significant events that were shaking and reshaping urban America: the ghetto flames of Watts and Detroit; the Civil Rights Movement; the Vietnam War; the Kent State killings; and even deeper, memories of Hiroshima and the Holocaust. So I then created a series of paintings depicting human forms with slashing brush strokes and intense colors to represent my anger. Unfortunately, most of these paintings were unwelcome at exhibits, and remain stored in my studio.

In the 1970s, as I gradually grew more in tune with and appreciative of Oregon's natural environment, I began a series of paintings called "Landscape, A Feminine Mythical View," which contained more gentle, flowing forms. Rivers, mountains, trees and the ocean became impregnated with monumental male and female forms that affirmed my personal joy of being and connections with family and friends.

Themes focusing on a multi-cultural world view entered my art during a sabbatical spent in India. There, despite the poverty, I found much stimulus and beauty in a culture where art, ritual and life are intertwined. Since then, as I have continued to travel alone each summer to many non-Western nations throughout the world, my paintings and etchings most often reflect universal themes, rites of passage, and mythology, as well as a sprinkling of symbolic political commentary.

As I look back over my Oregon years, I can identify three forms of networking that have significantly affected my development as artist, cultural researcher, and art educator. First, the grants that I obtained supported my world travels and forced me to develop the ability to share the results of my experiences through lectures and publications.

Second, I began to organize into thematic exhibits the drawings, paintings and prints that I produced during and after each journey, as well as photographs and collected examples of women's art. Some of these traveling exhibits gained broad exposure including "Impressions of India" (1972), and "Traditional Artists of Borneo and Sulawesi" (1984). I also began to package some of my own exhibits, including "China: An Outsider's Inside View," and "Impressions of Latin America."

The third significant impact upon my work has been the publication of my own paintings and prints in *Calyx.* Through the years, this has been a continuous source of pride, as well as the validation of the multi-cultural context of my art within the feminist art movement. Never fearful of "stirring a ruckus," *Calyx* has also published my drawings of Nicaraguan women in support of their revolution, and photographs of a little-known side of Nicaraguan women's contribution to society as artists and artisans.

I realized early in my career that I would never be commercially successful or accepted within the mainstream of American artists. However, through teaching I have gained the financial base to support my ongoing creative addiction. I consider the *Calyx* connection a vital emotional component of my survival as a woman and an artist. Through *Calyx* I also benefit from the shared visions of others as we each contribute our interpretations of yesterday and today, and our visions of what tomorrow can be.

*BETTY LADUKE*

NATIVE AMERICAN WOMEN'S ART AND
THE CONTEMPORARY MOVEMENT                    *GAIL E. TREMBLAY*

   The past ten years have seen the growth of an important movement in contemporary Native American art. Women artists have participated in this movement from the
very beginning, creating artworks that helped define what this movement is. It is an
expression of each artist's native vision in twentieth-century terms and a sign of our
ability to endure as native peoples who have no intention of vanishing from this conti-
nent or of allowing ourselves to become mere copiers of the powerful ancient works that
inspire us but do not express the totality of our experience today. Just as our ancestors
introduced new materials and concepts to create beadwork, button blankets, silver
jewelry, and wool rug designs after first contact and trade with Europeans, so contemporary native artists continue to introduce new materials and to create new art forms.
In the process, we create complex syntheses of influences from our cultural histories
and contemporary experiences where the art of the entire world is available to us for
inspiration. This opens up rich ideas about materials, techniques, and new ways to
express concepts that are important to us as native artists. It allows Lillian Pitt to use
raku or anagama firing techniques to make clay masks that express the legendary animals and stick Indians that populate her Warm Springs world. It also permits Edna
Jackson to take a traditional material like cedar bark and make cast paper masks with it
for incorporation into complex abstract compositions that talk about transformation.
   Women in our community have long been carriers of culture, producers of food
technologies, architects, designers, teachers, storytellers, medicine people and artists,
as have our men. But colonization by a patriarchal, European culture caused the work
of native *men* to be taken more seriously outside our communities. Until Euro-Americans
developed a vital women's art movement, native women's work tended to be devalued
and ignored by the art establishment, and it was difficult for women to make a living
from the production of fine art. There were rare exceptions like Pablita Velarde, the
most famous woman painter of the Santa Fe School, and her daughter Helen Hardin,
one of the first important woman painters of the contemporary Native American art
movement. Hardin began showing in the 1960s and by 1976 her work showed a developed sense of geometry. Works like "Mimbres Family Through Life," with its complex
series of interlocking shields and figures, were original departures from previous styles
of native art. In 1984, just before she died of cancer at 41, she began a series of etchings
entitled "Woman Series" which made significant departures from the old geometries,
and again Hardin was breaking new ground. But Helen Hardin, like her mother before
her, was unusual in her success at earning a living making art. Before 1980, many fine
artists became teachers or found other ways to contribute to the economies of their
people and could not devote as much energy to the production of fine art as they otherwise would have.
   It was not until this decade that a real flowering of Native American women's art
resulted in the development of the first contemporary Native American women's

exhibit, *Women of Sweetgrass, Cedar and Sage*. Curated by Jaune Quick-to-See Smith and Harmony Hammond, the exhibit is dedicated to Helen Hardin because of her ability to use native traditions as a foundation for contemporary art that expressed her personal vision.

In setting up this exhibit, Smith, a well-known native artist, was the primary contact person in the native community. She is one of the most important figures in the contemporary scene and has done much to promote the work of a large number of artists of both sexes. Hammond helped to found A.I.R. Gallery in New York City, one of the first and most important women's cooperative galleries in the country. Jaune and Harmony met when Jaune was a student in Harmony's class at the University of New Mexico where Jaune got her M.F.A. in painting. They discussed assembling a native women's exhibit and in 1983 decided it was time to bring attention to the work of the growing number of native women artists. They wrote grants, solicited slides and prepared to mount a major touring exhibit with a catalogue which would introduce people to the art and artists of the exhibit. Jaune contributed an article to the catalogue as did Erin Younger and Lucy Lippard, and each of the artists in the show produced a statement about her work. Younger, director of ATLATL, a native arts organization, did substantial work on many phases of the project and set up the touring schedule.

The result of all this work is an exhibit that opened in New York at the American Indian Community House Gallery and has been touring for two years. *Women of Sweetgrass, Cedar and Sage* has been written about in newspapers and magazines across the country and has made many people aware of the role of women in the contemporary Native American art movement. The accompanying catalogue is a permanent record of the exhibit. It has already been used as a college text and won the Fanny Lou Hammer Award. Unfortunately, it is out of print, and, as yet, there are no resources to reprint it.

By seeing *Women of Sweetgrass, Cedar and Sage*, you learn that it is impossible to stereotype native women's art, that innovation is important to the creative process of these women, and that each artist develops a personal aesthetic and a personal vision. For example, when a viewer examines the work of Jaune Quick-to-See Smith, she sees the rich gestural use of the brush tying together ancient pictographs and petroglyphs with abstract expressionist spontaneity of image. Jaune is fully aware of the ways in which native arts around the world influenced modernist and post-modernist movements in art, and her own close ties to the sources of those influences allow her to achieve a special perspective in her work. Mask maker Karita Coffey works in clay, a medium not used in mask making by her Comanche ancestors. She looks to African and Australian aboriginal art as well as Native American art for inspiration. Emmi Whitehorse does richly-colored aerial landscapes on which she scratches out symbolic landmarks seen around her grandmother's home.

One learns from looking at this show that native women are not interested in the divisions between art and craft, nor between printmaking, painting, photography, sculpture, beadwork, and basket weaving. This exhibit is not limited to a single medium but includes many. Where else could you see in one place Imogene Goodshot's beaded tennis shoes, Otellie Loloma's stoneware "Bird Woman" sculpture, Barbara Emerson

Kitsman's photograph of a strong contemporary Indian woman, Kay Walkingstick's painting with a thick impasto of pigment and wax, and Mary Adams's ash splint and sweetgrass basket. As a native person looking at this show, I see a universe of ways to make art inside the circle that keeps us whole. These relationships are rich and extremely important to me because they mean that other people's artificial divisions don't divide our power to relate to one another's work. As in traditional culture, each person is allowed the individual freedom to develop in ways that are best for the growth of those talents they have to share to make the community richer.

This exhibit has been a real breakthrough for Native American women artists, and hopefully, women will not let it fade from *her*story like so many of the achievements by women of color in *his*tory. Learning and recording the names and supporting the work of Native American women artists is yet another anti-racist and anti-sexist act that can change society. Knowing the names and the work of the thirty-one artists in this exhibit and other native women artists like Yeffe Kimball, Hulleah Tsinhnahjinnie, Leatrice Mikkelsen, and Jean La Marr is a powerful spell against the lie that women of color don't make important works of art. It is enriching to know this body of work is in the web of artwork by women of all colors because these works of beauty support life in this creation which Grandmother Spider is spinning into existence. When I remember I am one of these women among good friends making beauty on Mother Earth, I feel strong.

*GAIL E. TREMBLAY*

New York City, winter 1972. I'm sprawled out on the mattress that serves as bed and couch in our fourth floor studio apartment, crying. Somehow a secondhand copy of *The Second Sex* has found its way into my hands and I am reading and crying. I find the book hard going. I don't have the Freudian background for it, and I'm bothered by a lack I have no words for, a lack Gerda Lerner would identify for me years later as de Beauvoir's a-historical approach. But, for the first time in my nineteen years I've found something, something written down, that echoes my own conviction that things are very wrong between women and men. I cry for days. Finally, a little exasperated, my boyfriend says, "If it makes you that depressed, why don't you stop reading it?" So I do.

. . .

Portland, Oregon, winter 1976. I've dragged the chair over by the wood stove, where I sit surrounded by books. In the last week I've worked my way through *Radical Feminism, Beyond God the Father,* several issues of *Quest,* an old copy of Shulamith Firestone's *The Dialectic of Sex.* Once again I am crying. This is getting ridiculous, I tell myself. Joreen did not expect the "Tyranny of Structurelessness" to cause crying jags.

But I know something important is happening to me. I've been reading since I was six, I've put in my time and emerged from a college with a B.A. in theology, and now for the first time in my life I am becoming literate. For the first time, I am learning to read my own situation as a woman.

. . .

When *Calyx* first asked me to write an essay about the women writers and artists who've moved me most in the last ten years, I regretfully declined. I told Margarita that I'd been moved, indeed dragged, in so many different directions by writers and artists in those years, that I couldn't imagine writing about the process in any coherent way. I have so many literary heroes—Adrienne Rich, Audre Lorde, Barbara Deming, Alice Walker—how to make sense in a thousand words of the meaning of their diverse and precious work?

Then I began to think about another set of heroes, the women brave enough to read the work of these and other writers, to think about what it has meant to their own lives, and who are then brave enough to change those lives. The women and men who have risked and sometimes lost their lives (in this country and in others) to teach and to learn reading.

The schoolteachers I met in 1984 in Rosita, Nicaragua told me what it meant to teach adult education in the war zones there: you bury your books and pencils at dawn, so the *contra* won't find them in your house and kill you for being a teacher. At night you dig them up again, to teach another lesson.

In Nicaragua I first read Paolo Freire's almost impenetrable book, *Pedagogy of the Oppressed*, which describes how poor people can become readers and then political actors—the process of consciousness-raising. People learn to read, argues Freire, by reading about the things they know and the things that matter to them. Learning to read means learning to ask questions like, Why is there no potable water in this village? and, What can we do to change that?

After Somoza's fall, the FSLN's first national action was the *Cruzada de Alfabetización* —the Literacy Campaign. Three years after that campaign, I found myself living in a country where *conscientización* was going on all around me, where people were learning to read their own lives and ask their own questions. It seemed every other Nicaraguan I met was a poet. And eighty percent of those who learned to read in Nicaragua's campaign were women, because wherever people are illiterate, most of them are women.

Of course, I never really had to leave the United States in order to see the power of literacy in the lives of poor and working people. That history is all around us, although it's been stolen from us, and sometimes we've collaborated in the theft. Even among feminists, I think there's a tendency to devalue the actions of people who have thought about their situations enough to have articulated their politics. Somehow it's only the pure, inchoate reactions of the "innocent" that really count. Many people, for example, know the story of Rosa Parks, the Black woman who would not give up her seat on the bus to a white man, whose refusal touched off the Montgomery, Alabama bus boycott. Why is it that many fewer know that Rosa Parks's act of refusal was no sudden spontaneous combustion of exhaustion and frustration? Rosa Parks was an activist who had studied and continued to study with other activists at the Highlander Folk School in Tennessee. She had already thought long and hard about the situation of her people before she ever made that choice to keep her seat on that bus in Montgomery.

Any history of Black people in this country is in part the history of people willing to risk everything to learn and teach reading. One of the heroes of this history is Septima Clark. Clark, a Black woman from Charleston, South Carolina, served as education director at the Highlander Folk School, and helped set up Citizenship Schools in the south where Black people learned to read and write so that they could vote. Cynthia Stokes Brown has edited an extraordinary first person narrative, *Ready From Within* (1986, Wild Trees Press) in which Clark tells her story. Before she'd ever heard of Freire, Clark was using methods he described, teaching people to read what *they* wanted to learn, what *they* could use.

The more I believe in the centrality of literacy to real change in women's lives, the less I'm convinced of the primacy of language itself in making that change. When I first started reading feminist theory, I read as a poet. I had great hopes for the effects of changing language, and thus changing how people think. I knew that sexist English had really hurt me in my gut, made me invisible in countless debilitating ways. Eliminate the masculine generic, I hoped, and English speakers would be less inclined, even less able, to subsume women's experience under that of men.

It was Jan Clausen's classic essay, "A Movement of Poets," that first made me suspect that this emphasis on the power of language had given me a somewhat lopsided view of how change really happens. I had begun to confuse reflection with action, to confuse writing poems about office work with helping to mount an office workers' strike.

Liberation theologian Gustavo Gutiérrez describes his work as an asymmetrical combination of theory and practice, in which practice must always play the greater part. I think that's true: action without reflection may prove misguided and ineffective, but reflection without action is an exercise in futility, a kind of political masturbation.

Does that mean I think women should give up producing art and literature in favor of The Revolution? What good will all this literacy I'm pushing for do if there's nothing for us to read? A couple of years ago my father, a painter, told me I'd better give up revolution for art. "If you are serious about your poetry," he said, "you can't keep doing all this political work. You have to choose; you don't have time for both."

I love my father, but I think for once he's given me bad advice. Art and action have to drive each other. The more women risk, the farther we go, the more we will need both the impetus and the solace women writers and artists can give us.

REBECCA GORDON

This is my dialogue, my conversation, with certain French feminist thinkers whose voices sound so sweet, so strange in my ears that my hair stands on end, and hisses back . . . laughing.

From Christiane Makward I hear certain central words in the texts that concern *the inscription of femininity:* these words are open, non-linear, unfinished, fluid, exploded, fragmented, polysemic; incorporating lived simultaneity rather than following logical/sequential thought; differing from the preconceived, the oriented, and the masterly. My tongue curls around all these words as if they were big, juicy raspberries, but all the same I think that to define women's writing thus by its difference from men's writing is neofreudian (a word which I spit out like a stinkbug). If logos is law and order, if language is the Father('s), then the feminine is by definition silent, then the feminine is unspeakable. Thought excludes the feminine; there is no feminine thought. So what else is new? Woman does not exist, says Father Lacan, because *"elle ne se dit pas,"* she does not say herself. To follow this line that defines the feminine as silence, the irrational, the incoherent, spontaneous, powerless, is once again to reduce the woman to a minus, a negative, the non-man. So I hear Makward say: "By identifying discourse with power, and then rejecting both, women are resigning themselves to silence and nonspeech. The speech of the other will . . . speak *for* them and *instead of* them." As the other, arrogating all literature to himself, has been doing all along.

The Fathers' reductive definition of language as the Father('s) excludes as non-language, non-discourse, what is spoken by women and by children of both sexes, that is, the mother tongue. Women speak themselves in the mother tongue; and it is not discourse but intercourse. It does not run out; it runs between.

If the language of the Fathers is spoken by the Superego and is the Law, the Mind, the Mono-Log, then indeed the mother tongue is the body/the unconscious, and also it is daily give and take, colloquy, conversation. The economy of conversation, of relationship, is not definable merely as what can be excluded from Reason. It is not a minus, nor a negation, but a power. If the Mono-Log of the Father is power over, what the mother tongue speaks is power to, the power that, rather than controlling, enables; rather than closing, opens; finds "not the sum, but the differences . . . " says Hélène Cixous.

A snake arises from behind my ear and says, "Look! They are married—the Father-language and the Mother-tongue!" I see this as a very patriarchal marriage, at present. Children are continually being born to it, legitimate infants all, though the Father exposes the infant girls and frequently threatens to disinherit the boys, and the Mother tends to wring her hands and cry and say, "I just don't understand young people these days!" The offspring of this awful marriage are the works of prose and poetry, the works of literature, the babytalk men and women speak. The language of art belongs to the Fathers only under the rule of patriarchy, as a child belongs to its father, by coercion, co-optation, colonization, as part of the White Man's Burden. The Father's power is power over and he fears all that escapes, all that enables, all that answers. Don't talk back to Daddy.

Even Shelley takes his justification from the realm of government, saying poets are the unacknowledged legislators. But from the older anarchism of women Hélène Cixous replies: "Writing is precisely the very possibility of change, the space that can serve as a springboard for subversive thought, the precursory movement of a transformation of social and cultural structures." The word as art is not the law. Art is not the lawgiver's Mono-Log. We writing artists speak for ourselves and to other people, expecting and ensuring by our art that we will be heard; equally, we listen; what would we have to say if we did not listen? This is the subversive intercourse that Ruling Power fears, slipping the condom of censorship on the man's tongue, but locking the whole woman lifelong into a chastity belt, an Iron Maiden of silence.

As women write themselves body and mind they restore power to, they empower, a language that has, by its determination to exclude the feminine, castrated itself. They restore music to a language that has, by its effort not to hear women's voices, made itself deaf. By saying themselves, by listening, women are taking back to themselves what men claimed to possess, and so dispossessing themselves and their children of the demons that held them paralysed, turned to stone, in the long nightmare of a civilization founded upon misogyny.

*URSULA K. LE GUIN*

References:

Christiane Makward: "To Be or Not to Be . . . a Feminist Speaker," Hester Eisenstein and Alice Jardine, eds.: *The Future of Difference*. Rutgers University Press, 1980.
Hélène Cixous: "The Laugh of the Medusa," *Signs* I:4.
Elaine Marks and Isabelle de Courtivron, eds.: *New French Feminisms: an Anthology*. University of Massachusetts Press, 1980.

Somewhere between the emotional
and kinetic miniaturization
of the straight American woman,
and the pre-emptive gesture of the dyke

who claims the space but does not fill it,
I know my native female aspect.
Nativity is central
to a woman, a poet, and a Greek

who grew believing
mythology history and the farthest
geographies the peripheries
of her national reach.

Not only Alexander but Bouboulina
also was great, and fifteen when called upon
by her nature and circumstance
to stand and advance against the Turks.

In 1821 Bouboulina's poetry
passed information accurately,
coded in rhythm and rhyme,
from mountain to ravine to creek,

and the subservient-looking peasants who worked there.
The ancients were re-known exactly
through poetry and without it,
for us, nothing.

The song in the middle
of the tape I use while working on my clients
says "we're only as strong as who came before us . . ."
and I don't have the heart

to edit it,
though I dislike
lyrics during bodywork
as too much enlisting the conditioned

mind in an otherwise
direct communication between two biofields.
As I approach middle age, with the thrill,
more than unexpected, astonishing,

of having reached a mountain peak
after a decade's dawdling, accustomed
to leaning backward so
the stress seems natural,

and lifting my eyes over the edge
in the resigned manner ascribed to maturity,
prepared all life to feel the brief
prime pinnacle but grieving

the downtrod, another
forty or so, human nature
permit, bending forward, (this
incline and not osteoporosis the reason for

forthcoming wattles and slump),
only to witness a broad, horizon-reaching mesa,
full of brooks (in C major
for viola d'amore, the Greek poet said),

hills, low valleys, blooms, grasses,
and all the accoutrements of fauna a
pastoral metaphor can hold, an era broad, stable,
and, in its upright stance, eminently *humane.*

Calm, endurance, serenity,
the values urgently sought though the blasphemous
contradictions of an adolescence to mid-thirty
(until I lost all trace of girlhood from my face,

a friend said) clear
between heart and mind a threshing ground
where compassion, outrage and dignity
share breadth the sexual alone

had augured with its olive branch
let loose each time to fly.

*OLGA BROUMAS*

Our climb at day's end would begin on opposite sides of the street. Up the hill toward the city, our bodies straining diagonally. Her silhouette *con ese chongo largo* down her back made her look resolute. Acknowledgments across the street: an economic wave; a hello into the dusk. On reaching the top of the hill, we would turn our separate ways, and the night would gently fold over the street.

This was routine for a time. From the Student Union at the bottom of that Iowa City hill, we would trek to our respective apartments. We kept an odd but tender distance between us. Perhaps I was more preoccupied with my own long journey to Iowa than with bridging gulfs.

She grew up in Havana. Her mother was a schoolteacher; her father a lawyer. Her father worked secretly against the Batista regime, but as a Roman Catholic did not fare well with Castro's revolution. He did not join the Communist Party; he fell out of favor and into hard times. The family eventually decided on sending their two daughters to the United States. Power of attorney was given to Catholic charities, and the two sisters moved from a Miami camp to painful experiences at a Dubuque, Iowa institution. This was followed by various Iowa foster homes. At seventeen, she and her sister were reunited with their mother in Iowa. Her father, at the time, was imprisoned.

When I met her, she had a closed, private look. A look I recognized in the Mexican-Indian faces of the women in my family. That same look, I knew then, was hooked and locked into my very own cheekbones. Still, *esa mirada* would give way, at times, to an enfolding warmth in her eyes. And that slow-motion smile, drawing easily across her face, would make me immensely happy. In the years to come, her preference was for photographs that held her, for all time, open-faced, smiling widely, or at the crest of a hearty laugh.

These are some memories I hold of Ana Mendieta. We crossed paths as University of Iowa graduate art students in the early seventies. I had just begun my graduate program; she was about to complete hers. Ana had just stunned the Iowa City art community with her conceptual work on rape. One work brought the invited but unwarned multimedia workshop members to the sight of Ana in her blood-splattered apartment, tied to a table, nude from the waist down. She then went to Oaxaca, Mexico, where she did a roof-top work: her body covered with a bloodied sheet on which lay a cow's heart. At the time of her Oaxacan work, I was reeling from the impact of tragic news from my family: news of a brother pleading guilty to and sentenced for a rape, and for the murder of two women.

Ana Mendieta and I went our own ways. But through the years, her imagery would reach me as it did others, initially through the feminist press. After her early work, she embarked on her *Silueta* series, using varied materials and environments. *Siluetas* of the female figure were excised on earth and rock of the flat, hilly, mountainous, swampy terrains in Mexico, Cuba, and this country. Other *siluetas* were outlined by blasted gunpowder, lit candles, sparkling fireworks, and flowers adrift in water. In Mexico, once it was a nude Ana, cradled by an ancient Mexican stone grave; white, tiny flowers seemingly growing from her body. Her last works, more formal but still figural, used natural materials: tree trunks, roots, limbs, earth, sand infused with binders and mounted on wood.

Ana Mendieta's work was to leave an imprint on many of us. Her early works were exorcisms, burning one's sight with unrelenting viscera. The later works were of regeneration, healing, and transformation.

In a culture that invalidates women, human/cultural diversity, and art of conscience, we live as if exiled in our own home. Ana's work, at its best, insisted on wholeness and connection. As such, she said "no" to exile. In her essay, "Mexican American Women's Home Altars," Kay Turner spoke of grace being "felt in any accomplishment of bridging separations." Ana's work had the grace of artist and woman mediating between nature/culture, spiritual/concrete, secular/sacred, and historical/political.

Ana Mendieta's work was imbued with "mythological time." Octavio Paz perceived such time as "impregnated with all the particulars of our lives: it is as long as eternity or as short as a breath . . . ." In myth and ritual (as in the fiesta) Paz said, "'. . . time has no dates: Once upon a time . . . .'; 'In the days when animals could speak . . .'; and 'In the beginning . . . .' And that beginning, which is not such-and-such year or day, contains all beginnings and ushers us into living time where everything truly begins every instant."

Ana's roots were in her *tierra Cubana*. Her work may have been "charms against the evils of her deracination," as Lucy Lippard suggests of Ana's work in *Overlay*. My own Mexican-Indian roots sought the oases of her work. Among many memories: *esas curanderas* of my childhood re-emerged. The *curanderas* whose mounds of colored *polvos* lay out on that flat, hot-baked, south Texas earth. I would squat down to the mounds, exploring them first with a *palo de mesquite,* then with my own hands as if my strokes would loosen the truth from them.

The natural properties of the touchstones we carry, whether *tierras Cubanas, tierras Mexicanas,* create a peculiar *anima*. Ana had that *anima*. This *anima* is poignant and tough, all at once. It is the raft that survivors take to the shores. This *anima* is the sustenance for the winters of the soul in Iowa. For months, years there, one may hear not a word in one's mother-tongue. Did *I* survive on the word *murcielago*? Or was it *calavera,* or *molcajete,* spoken to myself in my room, doing a slow savor of each syllable?

Ana's work also tugged at what Lucy Lippard called "human racial memory" through the "restoration of symbolic probity." Those of us—brown, red, black, yellow, or white—who have not altogether forgotten, come to that memory. From my year spent in Arizona, this I remember: the Papago Friendship Dances behind San Xavier del Bac. Whites, invited to join the circle dance, were apprehensive, clumsy with the movements of the "perpetual spectator." Shy but thirsty, they would reach for the reconnecting thread. That is the human need with which many came to Ana's work.

For *all* that Ana gave us, her work was still the tender shoot of the young artist. More was yet to come. The mature work was yet to be done. She was eager to return to Rome; a venture initially made possible by the *Prix de Rome*. But the work will not be done. Ana Mendieta died at dawn, September 8, 1985. In the hothouse, early morning hours of that day, Ana fell from a thirty-fourth floor bedroom window of husband Carl Andre's Greenwich Village apartment.

Andre, who claimed it was suicide, was indicted on two counts of second degree murder. The district attorney cited "strong circumstantial evidence." This indictment was later overturned by a judge, claiming that "some of the evidence was inadmissible, and the jury instructions inadequate." However, the judge's opinion also stated that "it appears that there may remain sufficient evidence to sustain the indictment." Assistant District Attorney Martha Bashford, in charge of the case, reconvened a second grand jury, pressing for re-indictment. (At this time, this writer is unaware of this jury's decision.)

B. Ruby Rich, a friend of Ana Mendieta, speaks of her death as "a parable of the relative power of men and women in the art world." Loyalties, in a year of inactive indictment and no trial date, also fall on the fault lines of class, generation, and aesthetics. Andre, age fifty, is a founding figure of minimalism; its foundations pure, lean, and anti-symbolic. Many of Andre's supporters are of that generation. For "many women who came of age with the minimalists, brotherhood is outweighing sisterhood," according to Rich.

Whether murder, suicide, or accident, all strike me as monstrous, each in its own way. The heart is cleft. The truth must be known. Many of us have been saying goodbye to Ana. *Nos despedimos.* We do so in many ways: cradling her, assessing her work, examining our own lives. Some do so inwardly, quietly; some outwardly, defiantly. The filthy beast of silence has risen again. Her voice and ours muted. And the silence, of those fearing the established art world's wrath for speaking out, is loud.

This incongruent couple: North and South personified. What does one do with them? One partner lives; the other dead. Ana had immigrant baggage. Ana was Other: Ana of the discomfitting passions; Ana- euphoria; Ana of the alienating toughness; Ana-power, Ana-thema.

How does one, who called herself "Tropic-Ana," end up with a portly, rigid New Englander atop the glittering City; psyches ensnared? What did they seek—and find—in each other? I really want to know. Not ever for anecdote's sake, but to understand Ana. Because I want to know my own journey. Where do our journeys miscarry I need to know about the way home. The home of grace and authenticity; the home of the "self without estrangement."

*ADA MEDINA*

Translations:

*con ese chongo largo:* with that large twist of hair
*esa mirada:* that look
*tierra Cubana:* Cuban earth
*tierras Mexicanas:* Mexican earth
*curanderas:* healing women using folk medicine
*polvos:* powders, specifically pigments (in this case)
*palo de mesquite:* stick of mesquite wood
*anima:* spirit, mind, courage
*murcielago:* bat (mammal)
*calavera:* skull
*molcajete:* granular mortar and pestle for grinding chiles and spices, pre-Colombian in origin
*nos despedimos:* we say our farewells

References:

Kay F. Turner: *Lady-Unique-Inclination-of-the-Night,* Cycle 6, Autumn 1983. University of Texas, Austin, Folklore Center.
Octavio Paz: *The Labyrinth of Solitude,* Grove Press, Inc., New York.
Lucy R. Lippard: *From the Center,* E. P. Dutton, New York.
Lucy R. Lippard: *Overlay,* Pantheon Books, New York.
B. Ruby Rich: "The Screaming Silence," *Village Voice,* September 28, 1986.
Suzi Gablik: *Has Modernism Failed?* Thames and Hudson, New York.

# THE COORDINATING COUNCIL OF LITERARY MAGAZINES
## is pleased to announce the winners of
# THE 1986 GENERAL ELECTRIC FOUNDATION AWARDS FOR YOUNGER WRITERS

- **Julia Alvarez** for fiction published in **the new renaissance.**
- **Sandra Joy Jackson-Opoku** for fiction published in **Heresies.**
- **Rodney Jones** for poetry published in **River Styx.**
- **Ewa Kuryluk** for a literary essay published in **Formations.**
- **Jim Powell** for poetry published in **The Paris Review.**
- **Eliot Weinberger** for a literary essay published in **Sulfur.**

These awards honor excellence in new writers while recognizing the significant contribution of America's literary magazines.

This year's judges were: **Michael Anania, Thom Gunn, Elizabeth Hardwick, Margo Jefferson** and **Charles Simic.**

For information about The General Electric Foundation Awards for Younger Writers, contact: **CCLM, 666 Broadway, New York, NY 10012. (212) 614-6551**

# CONTRIBUTORS' NOTES

These notes also serve as an index. The form and page number of each contributor's work is in **boldface** at the end of each entry. *Note: Names followed by asterisks indicate entries that have not been updated. The bracketed dates following listings with asterisks refer to the year the biographical information was originally published.*

**MARJORIE AGOSIN**, a native of Chile, is a faculty member in the Spanish Department at Wellesley College. She is the author of six books, including her latest, *Scraps of Life: Women Under Pinochet* (Williams and Wallace, 1987). **Poetry, 115-116**

**PAULA GUNN ALLEN** teaches Native American and Ethnic Studies at the University of California, Berkeley. She has published four chapbooks, a book of poetry, a novel, and a widely acclaimed collection of essays, *The Sacred Hoop: Recovering the Feminine in American Indian Traditions* (Beacon Press, 1986). **Poetry, 77**

**JULIA ALVAREZ** is a poet and fiction writer. She is a recipient of the Third Woman Press Award in Fiction, the CCLM GE Younger Writers' Award (1986), and a National Endowment for the Arts Fellowship in Creative Writing (1987). Her work has been widely published. She teaches writing at the University of Illinois. **Poetry, 174**

**GURI ANDERMANN** "I am currently working as a legal assistant in a Tucson law firm and, consequently, have been too mired in legal machinations to write anything of interest." **Poetry, 11**

**BARBARA BALDWIN** was one of the founding editors of *Calyx*. Her poems have appeared in *Helicon Nine* and *Negative Capability*. She currently works as an editor for the Western Rural Development Center at Oregon State University. **Poetry, 72**

**ELLEN BASS** is the author of several books of poetry, most recently, *Our Stunning Harvest* (New Society Publishers). She is co-editor of *I Never Told Anyone: Writings by Women Survivors of Child Sexual Abuse* (Harper & Row, 1987) and co-author of a healing guide for survivors to be published in 1988. **Poetry, 32-33, 148-149**

**ZULEYKA BENITEZ\*** was born in the Panama Canal Zone and grew up in Europe, Central America, and the U.S.A. She teaches at Iowa State University and has a volume of narrative drawings published by Lost Roads Photography. [1981] **Art, 51**

**BETH BENTLEY** teaches a poetry workshop at the University of Washington. She has two collections of poems published by Ohio University Press, *Phone Calls From the Dead* (1971), and *Country of Resemblances* (1976). **Poetry, 30**

**SUJATA BHATT** was born in Ahmedabad, India in 1956. Her poetry has been published in the U.S.A., Ireland, and England and her first book of poetry, *Brunizem*, is forthcoming from Carcanet Press. She currently lives in Bremen, West Germany. **Poetry, 58-64**

**PEARL BOND** lives in Kingston, NY. Her work has appeared in numerous poetry journals and was collected in her book, *To Polish The Moon*. **Poetry, 114**

**OLGA BROUMAS** teaches at FREEHAND, a fine arts program for women she helped found in Provincetown, MA. Her most recent book is *What I Love, Selected Translations of Odysseas Elytis* (Copper Canyon, 1986). **Poetry, 146-147, 156-157; Essay, 235-236**

**CAROLYN CÁRDENAS** holds an M.F.A. from Drake University, where she did advanced studies of fifteenth century egg/oil tempera techniques. She has received numerous awards for her paintings which have appeared in galleries nationwide. Currently she teaches painting at the University of Nevada, Reno. **Art, 52**

**ANDREA CARLISLE** is the recipient of an Oregon Arts Commission Individual Artist Fellowship. Her fiction is included in *Editors Choice II* (The Spirit That Moves Us Press, 1987). Her first novel, *The Riverhouse Stories*, was published by **Calyx Books** in 1986. **Fiction, 183-195**

**CLAUDIA CAVE**'s paintings and drawings have been exhibited in New York City and throughout the Northwest. Her paintings have been published in *Mississippi Mud* and *Clinton St. Quarterly* and her work was included in the 1983 and 1985 Oregon Biennial exhibits. **Art, 53**

**MARISHA CHAMBERLAIN** is a playwright and poet as well as a fiction writer. Her play, *Scheherazade*, won the Dramatists Guild/CBS National New Play Award in 1984. A first book of poems, *Powers*, was published by New Rivers Press in 1984. **Fiction, 196-201**

**ELOUISE ANN CLARK** exhibits throughout Oregon. In 1984, she won an Award for Outstanding Achievement in the Field of Fine Arts from Women in Design International. She lives in McMinnville, Oregon. **Art, 96**

**JAN CLAUSEN** still lives in Brooklyn with her lover and their daughter. Her most recent book is a novel, *Sinking, Stealing* (Crossing Press, 1985). Her poetry, fiction, and criticism appear in a wide range of feminist and progressive publications. **Poetry, 73-74; Fiction, 122-131**

**JANET CULBERTSON** received art degrees from Carnegie Institute, Pratt Graphic Arts Institute, and New York University. Her work has been widely exhibited and is included in public collections including the Heckscher Museum of Art (NY), and the Fine Arts Museum, University of Massachusetts. **Art, 165**

**SHEILA DEMETRE** is a native of Seattle. She received her M.A. in Creative Writing from the University of Washington. Her poems have appeared in literary magazines including *Puget Sound Quarterly, Backbone,* and *Poetry Northwest.* **Poetry, 76**

**SHARON DOUBIAGO** is the author of the epic poem *Hard Country* (West End Press) and the recipient of two Pushcart Prizes. She recently completed *South America Mi Hija,* a 200-page poem to her daughter, and a collection of stories. **Poetry, 25-29**

**VICKI FOLKERTS-COOTS** received a B.F.A. from Oregon State University. Currently she is a graduate student at California College of Arts and Crafts where she is the recipient of a Ford Foundation scholarship. Her work has been exhibited in Oregon and California. **Art, 104**

**MARILYN FOLKESTAD** has been published in *Poetry Northwest, Mississippi Mud,* and others. Her first book of poetry, *Ghost Dancing,* was published in 1986 by Howlett Press in Portland, OR. She writes poetry, short stories, and plays. **Poetry, 120-121**

**PATRICIA FORSBERG** lives in Missoula, Montana with three fat cats, an old dog, and her spouse. In 1986 she lived in Italy and searched for art in Tuscan cities. Her paintings have been exhibited throughout the western U.S.A. **Art, 101**

**CAROL S. GATES** teaches Design/Visual Communications at the University of Oregon. Her most recent exhibits have been at the Portland Art Museum and at the Steirhead Gallery in Glasgow, Scotland. **Art, 16**

**PESHA GERTLER** lives in Seattle. She is co-founder of "Women's Voices and Visions" and teaches at the University of Washington and North Seattle Community College. Her work has appeared in many periodicals. Her most recent book is *The Mermaids and the Seated Women.* **Poetry, 178**

**DIANE GLANCY** had two collections of poetry published in 1986: *Offering* (Holy Cow! Press), and *One Age in a Dream,* which won the Lakes and Prairies Prize from *Milkweed Chronicle.* She has an essay in *I Tell You Now* (University of Nebraska Press, 1987). **Poetry, 68; Essay, 213**

**NATALIE GOLDBERG*** is the author of *Chicken and In Love* (Holy Cow! Press, 1980). She received a Bush Foundation Fellowship in 1983. [1983] **Poetry 152-153, 154-155**

**RENNY GOLDEN** is a founding member of the Religious Task Force on Central America. Currently she is completing a poetry manuscript based on her experience working with refugees in El Salvador and Guatemala. She also co-authored, with Michael McConnell, *Sanctuary: The New Underground Railroad* (Orbis Press, 1986). **Poetry, 41-43**

**REBECCA GORDON** is an editor of *Lesbian Contradiction: A Journal of Irreverent Feminism.* Her book, *Letters from Nicaragua* (Spinsters/Aunt Lute, 1986) chronicles the six months she spent working with Witness for Peace in that country. **Poetry, 151, 181-182; Essay, 230-232**

**KATHERINE GORHAM** is an artist and activist based in Eugene, Oregon whose work reflects her concerns regarding women's issues and the political situations in Central America and South Africa. She recently participated in a show at the Woman's Building in Los Angeles. **Art, 50**

**MARILYN HACKER** is the author of *Love, Death, and the Changing of the Seasons* (Arbor House, 1986), a lesbian novel in sonnets, and poetry collections *Assumptions* and *Taking Notice.* From 1982 through 1986 she was editor of the feminist literary magazine, *13th Moon.* **Poetry, 150**

**MARY HATCH** holds an M.A. in painting from Western Michigan University. Her work has been exhibited widely and she recently received a Michigan Council for the Arts Creative Artist Grant. **Art, 107**

**ESTER HERNANDEZ** is a Native Californian of Mexican ancestry. She graduated from U.C. Berkeley, has exhibited her work widely, and participated with *Las Mujeres Muralistas de San Francisco* (1974). She is the recipient of a California Arts Council Artist-in-Residence grant and currently directs printmaking and mural workshops at senior citizen centers in Oakland. **Art, 106**

**JANE HIRSHFIELD's** poetry has appeared in *The New Yorker, The Atlantic, The American Poetry Review,* and elsewhere. In 1985, she received a Guggenheim Fellowship. Her poetry is collected in *Alaya*, (The Quarterly Review of Literature Poetry Series, 1982). **Poetry, 13**

**LINDA HOGAN** teaches in the American Indian Studies program at the University of Minnesota. She is the author of several books, most recently, *Seeing Through The Sun* (University of Massachusetts Press, 1985). **Fiction, 132-140**

**ALEXA HOLLYWOOD\*** has been published in *Jawbone, Western Edge, Poetry Seattle* and *Bunchberries. [1980]* **Poetry, 12**

**SIBYL JAMES** teaches in the Seattle area. Her work has appeared in over 70 journals and anthologies in the U.S.A., Canada, England, and France. She has two books of poetry: *The White Junk of Love, Again* (**Calyx Books**, 1986) and *Vallarta Street* (Laughing Dog Press, 1987). **Poetry, 172-173**

**MEREDITH JENKINS** is one of the founding editors of *Calyx*. She lives in Seattle where she works in airbrush on over-size color photographs and is a production engineer for a printing firm. Her work has been exhibited widely, including shows in Florida, Texas, New York, and California. **Art, 160**

**TERRI L. JEWELL** is "a Black Lesbian Feminist—born in Louisville, KY on 10-04-54—applying to Michigan State for graduate work in social work and gerontology so that I can go back to my people, glean our wisdom and place our lives into the literature." **Poetry, 117**

**MAREAN L. JORDAN\*** writes both fiction and poetry and is a Ph.D. candidate in English Literature at the University of California, Davis. [1982] **Poetry, 70-71**

**FRIDA KAHLO** (1907-1954), a Mexican artist, taught herself to paint while convalescing from a 1922 accident that left her in pain for the rest of her life. She was married to muralist Diego Rivera and her work was overshadowed by his until she was "discovered" by the Parisian surrealists in 1939. **Art, 47, 105**

**PAULA KING\*** is interested in "developing stitchery as a political art form and as a celebration of the creative energy of generations of women who have not been considered artists." [1977] **Art, 23**

**BARBARA KINGSOLVER** lives in Tucson, Arizona. Her poetry and fiction are published in *Heresies, Sojourner,* and *The Virginia Quarterly Review*. She just completed her first novel and is awaiting the birth of her first child. **Poetry 36-38, 39-40**

**DEBORAH KLIBANOFF** studies nursing at Seattle University. She hopes to transform this experience, along with her love for documentary photography and her work with the elderly into "skillful services as part of actualizing the Dharma." **Photography, 206**

**FAEDRA KOSH** lives, teaches and makes art in Seattle. "My current obsession is how so many realities mutually co-exist in our universe and how we behave as if they don't." **Art, 14, 163; Essay, 218-219**

**BETTY LADUKE** is Professor of Art at Southern Oregon State College, Ashland, Oregon where she has initiated courses on "Women and Art" and "Multi-Cultural Arts." She is the author of *Companeras: Women, Art, and Social Change in Latin America* (City Lights, 1986). **Art, 108, 109; Essay, 224-226**

**JOAN LARKIN** is the recipient of a 1987 National Endowment for the Arts Writing Fellowship. She is the 1987 Poet-in-Residence for the New York Writers Community and teaches at Brooklyn College. Her most recent book is *A Long Sound* (Granite Press, 1986). **Poetry, 158**

**ROBIN LASSER\*** has work published in *Westwind Journal of the Arts* and is widely exhibited. [1981] **Photography, 20, 21**

**ELIZABETH LAYTON'S** work deals with the problems of growing old in America. Her self-portraits reflect the concerns of women, the hungry, the disillusioned and the hopeful. Her work is exhibited widely and has been featured in *Saturday Review, People, Art in America* and *Life,* among others. **Art, 55, 209**

**URSULA K. LE GUIN** is the author of over 30 books including novels, short story collections, poetry, criticism, and children's literature. Her novel *Always Coming Home* (Harper & Row, 1985) was a 1985 American Book Award runner-up. **Poetry, 34-35; Essay, 233-234**

**LI CHI** was born in 1902 in China. She has translated Wordsworth into Chinese and Hsu Hsia-k'o into English and her collected poems will soon be published in the People's Republic of China. **MICHAEL PATRICK O'CONNOR** was born in Buffalo and lives in the Great Lakes area. **Poetry, 78-79**

**LYN LIFSHIN** teaches poetry and prose writing at universities, colleges, and high schools throughout the Northeast. She has won numerous prizes and grants and her poetry has appeared in most poetry and literary magazines across the country and is collected in her book, *Kiss The Skin Off* (Cherry Valley Editions, 1985). **Poetry, 69**

**LINDA LOMAHAFTEWA** is Hopi/Choctaw and lives in Santa Fe, New Mexico where she is an instructor at the Institute of American Indian Arts. Her work is exhibited widely and is included in the "Women of Sweetgrass, Cedar and Sage" show that recently toured the U.S.A. **Art, 98**

**PAULA LUMBARD\*** lives and teaches in Los Angeles. She also lectures and has been published in *Woman's Art Journal* and *Pandora.* [1983] **Art, 99**

**YOLANDA MANCILLA** is the child of Cuban and Peruvian working-class parents and grew up in the eastern U.S.A. and Puerto Rico. Currently a Ph.D. student in Clinical/Community Psychology, she also teaches creative writing to Latin American immigrants and refugee adolescents in the Washington, DC, area. **Poetry, 65-66**

**GRAÇA MARTINS\*,** is a native of Portugal. She participated in the Graphic Arts Design course at the Art School of Portugal. Together with Isabel de Sa, she produces *Folheto,* a Portuguese feminist monthly. [1981] **Art, 46**

**DARLENE MATHIS-EDDY** is the author of *Leaf Threads, Wind Rhymes* (Barnwood Press, 1985) and has published widely including *Pebble, Cottonwood, Bitterroot,* and *Green River Review.* She teaches English at Ball State University. **Poetry, 118-119**

**COLLEEN McELROY** recently completed a novel during a sabbatical at the MacDowell Colony. She has two books to be published in 1987: a collection of poetry, *Bone Flames* (Wesleyan University Press); and a collection of short fiction, *Jesus and Fat Tuesday* (Creative Arts Books). **Poetry, 176**

**SANDRA McKEE** "lives in the shadow of the Williamsburg Bridge on the Lower East Side of New York City. She continues to paint while managing an art room for three magazines. McKee credits her stamina to vitamins and an occasional martini." **Art, 162**

**ADA MEDINA** is Xicana, born in Texas of working class parents. She currently is an Associate Professor of Art at Carnegie-Mellon University. She has exhibited widely, won awards, and been artist-in-residence at Yaddo (Saratoga Springs, NY). She participated in the exhibition "In Homage to Ana Mendieta" at Zeus-Trabia Gallery, NYC. **Art, 17, 18; Essay, 237-240**

**ANN MEREDITH** is a 38-year-old Lesbian photographer who has been documenting women's culture for seventeen years. In 1985 she traveled to Kenya as a photographer for the UN Conference on the Decade of Women. **Photography, 164**

**LINDA JOAN MILLER\*** produced art for nineteen years before sending her work out to be seen and touched by other people. Her experience as an organizer for the Women's Action for Nuclear Disarmament taught her that her voice—her vision—is real and legitimate. [1983] **Photography, 161**

**PAT MORA**'s two poetry collections *Chants* (1984) and *Borders* (1986) were published by Arte Publico Press. She has won numerous awards including the Southwest Book Award and is a recipient of a Kellogg National Fellowship. She is Assistant to the Vice President for Academic Affairs at the University of Texas at El Paso. **Poetry, 179-180; Essay, 214-215**

**RONNA NEUENSCHWANDER** continues to do ceramic sculpture in Portland, OR. She is the recipient of an Oregon Arts Commission Individual Artist Fellowship and has been an Artist-in-Residence in Oregon schools. Since visiting Africa, she has concentrated on incorporating Third World concerns in her art. In 1987 she will return to Africa for a year. **Art, 167**

**ANNE NOGGLE** "In the fall of 1986 I went to the reunion of the Women Airforce Service Pilots, WWII (WASP) and photographed 220 of my fellow pilots. I am in the process of printing these images now. Mills College, the Museum of Modern Art, Ohio State University and the University of Oregon have added my photographs to their collections." **Photography, 202, 205**

**SHARON OLDS**'s latest book is *The Gold Cell* (Knopf, 1987). She is the recipient of numerous awards including the 1984 Lamont Prize, the 1984 San Francisco Poetry Center Award and the 1985 National Book Critics Circle Award. She teaches at NYU, Brandeis University, and Goldwater Hospital (Roosevelt Island, NYC). **Poetry, 8-9**

**CAROL ORLOCK**'s first novel, *The Goddess Letters*, is published by St. Martin's Press (1987). She has work forthcoming in the *Women of Darkness* anthology (Tor Books) and *Crossing the Mainstream/New Fiction by Women Writers* (Silverleaf Press). **Fiction, 80-84**

**PAULANN PETERSEN**'s poems have appeared recently in *Calapooya Collage 10, Hubbub, Sequoia,* and *CutBank.* She is currently a Stegner Fellow in Poetry at Stanford University. **Poetry, 175**

**JOANNA PRIESTLEY** is working on an animated film titled *She-Bop* about women, spirit and power. She teaches Film History at the Pacific Northwest College of Art and likes to lie naked in the sun and think about things. **Art, 22**

**MARGARET RANDALL** is still fighting to remain in the United States as the government seeks to deport her. Her publications are numerous and her latest books are *Albuquerque: Coming Back to the USA* (New Star, 1986) and *This is About Incest* (Firebrand, 1987). **Photography, 203, 204**

**CELESTE REHM** has had numerous solo and group exhibitions and her work has appeared in anthologies including *Super Realism: A Critical Anthology* (E.P. Dutton) and *Super Realism* (Orbis Publishing). She teaches at the University of Colorado. **Art, 15**

**MARY RILEY** "I am living and working in Greencastle, Indiana, no wiser or richer, but much grayer." **Art, 97**

**RENÉE ROMANOWSKI\*** studied Fine Arts at Moorpark College and the Portland Art Museum School. She taught in the Artist-in-the-Schools program in Oregon. [1982] **Art, 208**

**WENDY ROSE** is Hopi/Miwok. Her most recent book of poetry is *The Halfbreed Chronicles and Other Poems*, published by West End Press in 1985. **Poetry, 75**

**LIZA von ROSENSTIEL** is currently showing at the Davidson Galleries and Traver Sutton Gallery in Seattle. "Figures, color and psychological impact play an important role in my work." **Art, 168**

**PAULA ROSS** relocated to Southern California from New York. Recent shows include "Homage To Grandma Sophie" at the NY Historical Society (1986) and at the Museum of Immigration at the Statue of Liberty (1985). **Photography, 54**

**LAUREL RUST**'s poetry has appeared in *Common Lives/Lesbian Lives* and *Fine Madness*. She is embarking on a life as a nomad in the Southwest with her lover, their animals, a '65 Plymouth Valiant, and manual typewriters. **Prose, 85-95**

**SILVIA SANTAL** has exhibited in shows and competitions throughout the U.S.A. In 1985, her work won first place in "Enfoque Femenil" at the Guadalupe Cultural Arts Center in San Antonio. She is currently working with computer generated graphics and digitized photography. **Photography, 159**

**DEIDRE SCHERER** was selected as an Artist-in-Residence by the Vermont Council on the Arts after receiving her B.F.A. from the Rhode Island School of Design. Her work has been exhibited throughout the Northeast. **Art, 211**

**MONICA SJOO**, born in Sweden, now lives in England where she has been active in the Women's Movement since 1969. Her book, *The Ancient Religion of the Great Cosmic Mother of All* (Rainbow Press, Norway, 1981), co-authored with Barbara Mor, will be published by Harper & Row in 1987. **Art, 102**

**M. ANN SPIERS**, poet and playwright, wishes *Calyx* a Happy Birthday! **Fiction, 141-145**

**DANA LEIGH SQUIRES** is living in the Solomon Islands (Guadalcanal) as a Peace Corps volunteer. She is represented by Traver Sutton Gallery in Seattle. **Art, 166**

**JENNIFER STABLER-HOLLAND** lives in Uniontown, Washington, and has exhibited widely throughout the Northwest. Her work was included in "Living With the Volcano: The Artists of Mt. St. Helens," a traveling exhibit which toured the West from 1983 through 1985. **Art, 100; Essay, 220-221**

**JUDITH STEINBERGH** has published two books: *Lillian Bloom, A Separation,* and *Motherwriter* (both Wampeter Press), and co-authored, with Elizabeth McKim, *Beyond Words, Writing Poems with Children.* She is Poet-in-Residence in Brookline, Massachusetts. **Poetry, 10**

**ALFONSINA STORNI** was the first woman to enter the public literary world in Argentina. She wrote plays, articles and essays, as well as seven books of poetry before she died in 1928. **ALMITRA DAVID** is the recipient of a Pennsylvania Council On the Arts Fellowship in Poetry. Her poetry is collected in *Building the Cathedral* (Slash & Burn Press, 1986). **Poetry, 170-171**

**MARY TALLMOUNTAIN\*** "I was at a Spirit Camp for children in the wilderness of the Chilcoot, and I knew this was the land of my roots, this mystical, magical Alaska. Though I've spent most of my life in San Francisco, part of me has been in that unspoiled, clean place. I think we all have a retreat for our spirits, somewhere." [1986] **Poetry, 111**

**BARBARA THOMAS** lives in Seattle where she is a painter and a staff member of the Seattle Arts Commission. She exhibits her work in regional and national shows. **Art, 48, 49; Essay, 222-223**

**MELANIE TOLBERT\*** received her B.A. from Lewis and Clark College and studied at the Museum Art School in Portland, Oregon. [1982] **Photography, 19**

**CHARLEEN TOUCHETTE** lives and paints full time in Tuba City, Arizona. Her work was included in the "Women of Sweetgrass, Cedar and Sage" exhibit and at the Judah Magnus Museum in Berkeley. She will have a one-person show in Sacramento in the fall of 1987. **Art, 103**

**GAIL TREMBLAY\*** is Onandaga Mic Mac. She teaches at Evergreen State College. She is widely published and has two poetry books, *Night Gives Woman The Word* and *Talking To The Grandfathers.* [1984] **Poetry, 67; Essay, 227-229**

**INGRID WENDT** works as a visiting writer in Oregon's Artist-in-Education program. Her latest book of poetry is *Singing The Mozart Requiem,* (Breitenbush Books, 1987). She co-authored, with Elaine Hedges, the anthology *In Her Own Image: Women Working in the Arts* (The Feminist Press and McGraw-Hill). **Poetry, 112; Essay 216-217**

**MARTHA E. WEHRLE (DIBBLE)** recently spent a year studying ink painting in Japan. Her work is exhibited nationally, including a two-year traveling show in Texas called "New American Talent," and was exhibited at Expo '86 in Vancouver, B.C. She lives and teaches in Corvallis, Oregon. **Art, 210**

**ELEANOR WILNER** spent two years teaching at Temple University Japan in Tokyo. In 1987 she is Visiting Poet at the University of Chicago, and at the University of Iowa. Her awards include the Juniper Prize for Poetry. Her most recent book, *Shekhinah,* was the

1984 selection of the Phoenix Poets Series (University of Chicago Press, 1984). **Poetry, 44-45, 57**

**MYRNA YODER** "Since graduating from Oregon State University I've spent two months traveling in the Philippines and have held several odd jobs. Right now I'm in the process of applying to graduate school and plan to spend the next few years in intense printmaking study." **Art, 207**

**ANNE YOUNG** (pseudonym) has two grown sons and lives with her husband in Washington State. Her poetry is published in *Kansas Quarterly, The Literary Review, Southern Poetry Review* and *The International Women's Peace Anthology,* among others. **Poetry, 31**

**JANA ZVIBLEMAN** writes, teaches, edits, and mothers in Corvallis, Oregon. She is the winner of a 1986 Academy of American Poets Award. **Poetry, 113**

# EDITORS' NOTES

**DEBI BERROW** recently worked with Diane Thies to bring together a national women's art show, "Past Presence, A Circle of Women's Visions." She studied at Gray's School of Art in Scotland for a year, and received her B.F.A. from Oregon State University in 1985. She has been the Managing Art Editor for *Calyx* since 1984, and also does her own artwork at home whenever she can.

**LISA DOMITROVICH** has been working at *Calyx* since 1983. She loves feminist publishing and could hardly imagine doing anything else.

**MARGARITA DONNELLY** is a founding editor of *Calyx* and also works as an editor for ERIC Clearinghouse at the University of Oregon. She received a CCLM editors grant in 1985, and began serving on the CCLM Board in 1986. She is active in the struggle for justice and peace in Central America and in the world. Born in Venezuela, she is still not used to the "cold" North.

**CATHERINE HOLDORF** "Dismayed by the consumption and waste I witnessed while growing up in 'middle' America, I spent several years journeying through Third World countries in search of 'a more meaningful existence.' The discovery that quality of life is a matter of perspective rather than location brought me back to the U.S.A. where I happened on Corvallis and my husband, a motivated partner in the raising of vegetables, buildings, three children, and our collective spirit."

**SUSAN BATEMAN LISSER** is a writer, teacher, and mother of two children. She began volunteering for *Calyx* in 1986 and is in charge of book reviews for the journal.

**CHERYL McLEAN** has been an editor at *Calyx* since 1979. She is currently in production on her first book, *Oregon's Quiet Waters: A Guide to Lakes for Canoeists and Other Motorless Boaters*.

**CAROL PENNOCK** was desperately seeking a way to use her college degree when she stumbled upon *Calyx*—what a relief! there is life after receiving a B.A. in English. She misses her friends and family, who live in various parts of the country, but finds solace in the wonderful friendships she has gained through *Calyx*.

**LINDA VARSELL SMITH**, a freelance editor, writer, and graphic designer has published poetry in *Poet Lore*, *Lip Service*, and other small magazines. She has been a teacher and poet-in-the-schools and is currently working on a series of fantasy novels for children.

*The current editorial collective would like to thank all the members of past editorial boards who worked with* Calyx *during the past ten years. Their names are too numerous to list in this limited space, but it is important to understand that* Calyx's *history includes the talents, energy, and inspiration of a large group of volunteer editors who have helped* Calyx *flourish and blossom into her second decade. Thank you!*

Publication costs for this issue were funded in part by grants from the National Endowment for the Arts, the Oregon Arts Commission, and by donations from the following individuals: MATRONS: Effie Ambler, Patricia McMartin Enders, Jean Grossholtz, Joan Hoffman, Adele K-Smith, Deborah L. Perry, Judith Stitzel, Phyllis Stokes, Anne Wittels; DONORS: Anonymous, Genevieve Beach, Jan-M-Bell, Dr. Betty Bernard, Helen Marie Casey, Major N.V. Chenausky, Ann M. Davis, Mabel A. Dilley, Beverly Forsyth, Jean Grossholtz, Margaret Lumpkin, Patricia H. Mayo, Camille Patha, Anne Scheetz, Kathleen Sullivan. Thank you!

Special thanks to: Vanessa Jorgensen for production assistance; Stover & Sinclair for donation of accounting services; Karen Theiling, Claudia Keith, and, especially, Nancy Chapin for computer related assistance; Norma Remington for organizational skills and her energy; and Martha Cone for finding this retrospective a lovely and appropriate name.

**SUBMISSION POLICY:** *Calyx* accepts submissions of essays, short fiction, poetry, visual art, interviews, reviews, and critical essays. Please query for review list and guidelines. Prose, 5000 words; poetry, 6 poems; visual art, 6 slides or black and white photos. Include a brief biographical statement, SASE, and your phone number. *Calyx* assumes no responsibility for submissions received without adequate return postage, packaging, or proper identification labels. We only respond to queries accompanied by an SASE and do not accept submissions with postage due.

**SUBMISSION DEADLINES:** Between April 1 and August 1, 1987, *Calyx, A Journal of Art and Literature By Women* will not be accepting any manuscripts or art submissions. Beginning August 1, we will be accepting submissions until November 15, 1987 for the Spring 1988 issue. Please query with an SASE for further deadline information.

**PUBLICATION SCHEDULE:** Volume 11#1, a general-theme single issue will be published in Summer 1987. Volume 11#2&3 (late Fall 1987), will be the double issue Asian-American anthology. Volume 12#1, a single issue, will be released in Spring 1988 after which we hope to be back on a regular 3 issue/ year schedule. Our apologies to those inconvenienced by our recent unortho- dox publishing schedule.